CLAY BRENTWO
CINCH MOUNTAIN

Creative Texts Publishers products are available at special discounts for bulk purchase for sale promotions, premiums, fund-raising, and educational needs. For details, write Creative Texts Publishers, PO Box 50, Barto, PA 19504, or visit www.creativetexts.com

CINCH MOUNTAIN
by Jared McVay
Published by Creative Texts Publishers
PO Box 50
Barto, PA 19504
www.creativetexts.com

ISBN: 9780692195833

CINCH MOUNTAIN
By
JARED MCVAY

An imprint of Creative Texts Publishers, LLC
Barto, PA

This book is dedicated to my lady, Jerrilyn Burr. She is a valuable part of my life.

Thank you to all of my readers and your wonderful reviews. As long as you keep asking for more, I'll keep writing them… Through you I continually gain new readers and make wonderful new friends. I would also like to thank my publisher, Dan Edwards at Creative Texts Publishers, for having faith in me…

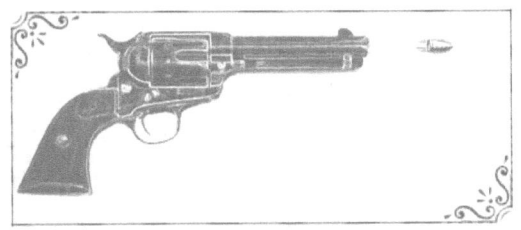

CHAPTER ONE

-

Loralie Benson had been extremely lucky, but then again, she hadn't been looking to strike it rich like the other gold seekers. She just wanted enough to rebuild her place back in the mountains of Tennessee. The Mullins had killed her folks and burned their place down, and tried to make it look like an Indian attack, but Loralie knew different.

As long as she could remember, the Mullins had been trying to figure a way to get their hands on Benson land, all three thousand acres of it, which amounted to a mountain full of good timber.

Life on Cinch Mountain had been hard, but it was her home and she wasn't about to give it up without a fight. Her pa had always said, "Loralie, this piece of the mountain is our'n and it's all we got. It's good timberland and there'll be folks want'n ta take it from you when I'm gone so's they can cut it down an get rich off'n it, but I'm ah hopin' you won't let'm. You jest remember the things I try ta teach ya girl. You can make ah good livin' raisin' horses and cattle thout destroyin' the trees or the land. Ownin' good land like this is everthin'. Thout land, ah person is nuthin'. You remember that, girl."

It was the last words her father ever spoke to her. A few hours later, she had gone off on a hunting trip to get a fresh supply of meat, and three days later when she returned, she found her mother and father lying in the yard, dead, with their scalps taken to make it look like Indians had done it. Indians might have stolen the horses and burned the place down, but they wouldn't have taken the cows, pigs and chickens. That was white man'si doings.

After burying her folks, she vowed to honor her papa's wants, but to do that; she would need a good bit of money, and the only place she knew of to get that kind of money was the gold fields of Colorado.

The only thing she had was her rifle, her handgun and the big Morgan horse her pa had won in a poker game.

She worked the rivers and inlets in the southeastern region of Colorado and found a small amount of gold, but not enough to make the trip worthwhile, nor to do what she needed done.

A few weeks later, up near Cherry Creek, she found a curve in the river that to the best of her reasoning had been overlooked. It was almost like picking apples off the ground; there seemed to be a nugget under every rock she turned over.

Knee deep in the cold water she panned the river bottom, and after sloshing it around, she would pick out two or three nuggets almost every time. After two weeks of working the Cherry Creek area, she figured she had enough gold to rebuild her home, with some left over to buy a few horses and cows to get started again, and maybe enough left over to last her several years down the road until the place started paying off.

The sun was shining brightly overhead and a young oriole, perched on a limb some twenty feet away from Loralie's camp, was trying on her newly found singing voice.

Loralie sat in front of her tent transferring gold nuggets from a wooden box into a leather pouch she'd brought with her. She smiled and said to herself. "I've done what I come ta do and now it's time ta go home and start rebuildin' my life."

She whistled along with the young oriole as she emptied the last of the nuggets into a leather pouch from the box where she'd kept them.

Thirty feet from where Loralie sat, two sets of eyes spied on her from just inside the tree line; eyes that held no friendship. Enzo Babineaux was pure evil and had no qualms about stealing other people's money, gold, horses, food or anything else of value.

Born and raised in the swamps of Louisiana, Enzo Babineaux had a full beard and brown, dirty, matted hair that hung down over his shoulders. His skin was the color of leather and his teeth were uneven and tobacco stained. In his bare feet, Enzo stood six foot six and weighed more than three hundred pounds. He could neither read nor write and had no desire to learn. There was a mean streak in him a mile wide and he had a hair trigger temper. Because of his size and short fuse, people tended to step wide of him and that's the way he liked it.

He had a veracious appetite for the opposite sex. Raping women and young girls was at the top of the things he liked to do; but when no females were available, small boys and young men were not to be excluded.

Enzo's mouth salivated as he watched the healthy looking young woman with the fiery red hair putting gold nuggets into a leather pouch. She had no hat on and her red hair glistened in the sunshine. He would take his time with this one, he thought to himself. He would make her scream and beg for him to let her die. He enjoyed it best when they begged.

"When I'm done with you, little lady, I'll gladly slit yer throat, but until then I'm gonna have me some fun," he muttered to himself. "Then, I'm gonna take yer gold, yer tent, and that good lookin' horse you got tethered over yonder," he said, nodding his head toward the big Morgan stallion.

The man standing next to him, Ira Broomfield, was a total opposite. Ira was raised by God-fearing parents back in Ohio and had been taught to respect people, especially women. He could read, write and do his sums well enough to have been a merchant, or even a schoolteacher, but that never happened. Fate seemed to have other plans, and delighted in making his life a living hell.

Ira was barely five feet tall and weighed one hundred and one pounds. He was small like his mother. He had blond hair and blue eyes and a petite body. As a child, he had been bullied and beaten on by the other boys and even a few girls, and by the time he turned sixteen he was at his wits end.

One day after being bullied by several boys and a mean-spirited girl, he stole a pistol from a local store and hunted each one down and shot them dead. When he got home, his mother saw the splatters of blood on his clothes and asked him about it, and when he didn't answer, his father grabbed him by the front of his shirt and began slapping him all about his face, yelling at him to answer his mother.

The anger inside him rose up like an erupting volcano. He pulled the pistol from his pocket and shot them both.

After going through his father's pockets, Ira found sixty-one dollars and a gold pocket watch. Ignoring the two dead bodies, he packed a few clothes and filled a sack with food. Before leaving, he poured kerosene on the floor, furniture, and his parent's bodies, then set fire to the house.

From the westbound boxcar he was riding in, Ira could see smoke rising above the trees from his parent's burning house and felt no remorse.

Six months later, he was broke and starving when Enzo found him lying in an alley in New Orleans. The young, girlish looking man stirred something inside Enzo. He liked his looks and took him home with him. During the next two years, the big man kept him hostage and molested him when he couldn't find a female.

After being molested by Enzo, Ira would sometimes sit in the corner of the room and cry himself to sleep, wishing he was dead.

Ira hated Enzo for what he'd made of him and wanted to kill him, but on the other hand, he had become attracted to him. It was weird, but being with Enzo Babineaux was as close to being loved, as he'd ever known. Ira was weak and he knew it. He also hated himself for it, but it was what it was. When Enzo headed for the goldfields, he took Ira with him, and Ira went along without a struggle.

Ira looked over at Enzo and saw the eagerness in his eyes and the saliva dripping from his mouth and knew the young lady didn't have long to live.

From all outward appearances, you would never know that Loralie knew someone was spying on her.

The big Morgan she rode had raised his head from where he stood eating grass and lifted his ears, letting her know that someone or something was nearby.

Pretending to scratch her leg, she pulled the leather thong off the hammer of her thirty-two-caliber pistol, and then resumed her work, eyes and ears alert to danger.

If someone was going to sneak up on Loralie Benson, he'd better be Injun good or he wouldn't make it, she thought to herself. She'd been raised in Tennessee, up on Cinch Mountain, with six brothers who were all good hunters and hell on wheels when it come ta fightin'.

Loralie had been raised like a boy and was as good a shot as any of her brothers and almost as good as her pa before he was killed by those back shootin' Mullins.

Three of her brothers had gone off to the war and had been killed by the Yankees. The other three had taken off for California and hadn't been heard from since. Maybe they were alive, or maybe not. It didn't matter. Any way she looked at it, the land was hers to look after and she meant to do what she could.

Being a mountain girl, and not knowing much about the weight or price of gold, she had no idea how much money her sack full of nuggets was worth, but she did know that a leather pouch that took two hands ta lift, was worth a fair amount of money; more than enough to do what she needed to do. She also knew there were a lot of men who would murder her to get her gold and never think twice about it, or even lose any sleep, for that matter.

She heard a noise and dropping her right hand down next to her gun, she looked toward the forest. Coming out of the trees, Loralie saw a small, frail looking man walking in her direction. He had long, blond hair, and was wearing ragged, dirty clothes that were too big for him, but he carried no weapon of any kind that she could see.

"Hello the camp," the young man said in a high pitched, woman's sounding voice.

Loralie relaxed and moved her hand away from the butt of her pistol, but still in easy reach if need be. "Hello, yerself. Come on in and sit. Got coffee on if'n you'd like some."

"Thank you, that would be nice," the young man said as he walked toward the coffee pot sitting on a flat rock at the edge of the fire.

Loralie looked around, and even though she saw no one else, her sixth sense told her there was more to this than met the eye. Her gut told her the young man wasn't alone. Through her peripheral vision, she watched the big Morgan. Her papa had set ah site of trust in the horse, and so did she. His head was now turned toward a different part of the forest.

Loralie had learned long ago to depend on the big horse and turned her body slightly so she could see in the same direction he was looking. At first, she saw nothing, but her pa had taught her to not look at what she expected to see, but to look for what might be in the shadows. Sure enough, she saw the outline of what appeared ta be ah good-sized man, just inside the trees. She watched as the outline moved away from where she was looking.

Enzo had seen her turn and decided to move to a better hiding place. He didn't want her to see him coming when he made his move. He'd wait for Ira ta distract her, like he'd been told to do.

"Go ahead, pour yerself ah cup of coffee," Loralie said to the young man, as she turned and walked toward her tent. "There's a cup sittin' there by the pot. Careful now, it might be hot."

Carrying the bag of gold in both hands, she moved toward the tent, but her eyes never left the shadow in the trees.

When she reached her tent, she stepped inside and dropped the bag of gold onto her soogun, then grabbed her Winchester lever action rifle, and came back outside. She threw the butt of the rifle to her shoulder, jacked a bullet into the chamber and squeezed the trigger in the direction of whoever was hiding in the trees.

She had given the person in the trees no warning, figuring he was here to steal her gold and more than likely try to do her harm. She purposely aimed low. She didn't want to kill anybody, just let him know she was not some defenseless female who could be run roughshod over.

The shadow let out a scream and lunged into the clearing, his eyes ablaze with anger, a bloodstain already showing on his left pant leg.

Loralie stepped back and her mouth flew open. She'd seen some big men up on the mountain, but nothing to compare with this monster. One bullet would hardly slow a man like him down, especially only being shot in the leg.

She took a quick glance in the direction of the young man who'd come into her camp and saw him standing next to the fire, wide eyed and scared. There was a wet spot on the front of his pants and it wasn't spilled coffee.

Looking back at the monster of a man who was charging in her direction, arms spread wide like an angry bear, Loralie took a deep breath and sighted down the barrel of her rifle, then began pumping lead into his chest cavity as fast as she could jack shells into the chamber and squeeze the trigger. It took six shots to the heart; all within a spot no bigger than a silver dollar before the big man stopped approximately five feet from her. He stood looking at her for what seemed to be a long time before he fell over backward.

He landed, spread eagle, flat on his back. The earth beneath Loralie's feet shook like an earthquake tremor.

She hated killing, but she had no choice. He would have killed her and God only knows what else. It was just like back home, kill or be killed. She hoped someday things could be different. She'd like to live like one of them ladies she read about in the books pa had brung home.

Loralie swung the rifle in the direction of the small, girlish like man and saw he hadn't moved.

"You plan on tryin' somethin' stupid?" Loralie asked.

After swallowing several times, he finally found his voice. "No ma'am. I didn't like doing this in the first place, but he made me," Ira said, pointing at the now dead monster, Enzo Babineaux.

Ira looked over at the man who repeatedly molested and beat him and gave a sigh of relief. It was finally over. The monster would never abuse him again. "Thank you," he said to the woman with the shiny red hair. Tears were running down his face.

It didn't take long for Loralie to recognize what the relationship between the two men had been. She could almost feel sorry for the young man, but not quite. She didn't understand his kind and never would.

Her thoughts were interrupted by the young man's strangled voice.

. "Will you allow me to go through his pockets? He never let me to carry any money, and now that I'm alone…"

Loralie thought for a moment, then nodded her head. "Go ahead, but watch yerself, I'll be keepin' an eye on ya, so don't try nuthin' stupid."

Ira hurried over to Enzo and began going through his pockets. Just touching him brought back memories, some of pain and some of joy. His mind was a whirlwind of questions. Who would take care of him now that Enzo was dead? Where would he go, what would he do?

He was ashamed of what he'd become, but without Enzo to protect him, he would be at the mercy of everyone he came in contact with. It would be just like it was before he met Enzo. His only means of employment would be some house of ill repute where some of the clients preferred young men to the girls.

Inside Enzo's coat, Ira found a small hideout gun in a holster, a single shot derringer. Ira knew that he used it on women to frighten them before he raped them. He also knew Enzo's favorite way of killing them was to skin them alive and listen to them scream.

Loralie turned and was walking toward the fire as Ira reached in and pulled out the twenty-five-caliber hideout pistol.

Once again, Loralie saw her horse's head come up and she whirled, pulling her pistol from its holster.

Ira was lifting the small pistol from its hiding place when he saw the woman whirl.

Instead of pointing the derringer at her, he placed the end of the barrel in his mouth and before she could stop him, he pulled the trigger.

Loralie stood there for a long moment, stunned by what the young man had done. She could understand them wanting to rob her of her gold; that would put them on easy street, but to kill hisself like that; well that was more than her mind could consider.

After rolling the two dead men into a ditch and piling rocks over them so the wolves and other critters wouldn't get at them, she stood for a moment, wondering if she should say something but nothing came ta mind.

Finally, she turned, struck her camp, and then tied it onto the back of the burro she'd gotten off a man who had given up on striking it rich. He told her he was going back to Indiana and she could have the burro, tent and all for twenty dollars.

Before he left, he warned her that she was chasing a fool's dream, but she had her own plans and they didn't include giving up before she'd even tried.

When she stepped into the stirrup and swung her leg over the big horse, he began to move away from the camp, not liking the smell of death. The burro was on a long lead rope and followed ten feet behind.

She searched the nearby area for the two men's horses and when she didn't find any, she decided they must have come from the freight train that had gone by a few hours before. The railroad tracks were less than half a mile from her camp.

Later that evening, Loralie Benson was sitting next to a small fire built in a shallow hole she'd dug with her knife so it would be hard for anyone but herself to see, enjoying a cup of coffee. She had decisions to make. Her first inclination was ta hightail it back to Tennessee.

Before leaving for the gold fields, she'd told the sheriff back there what her plans were and that she would be back as soon as she could. She'd asked him if he would keep an eye on the place until she got back, and he'd said he would. She didn't want the Mullins saying the land had been abandoned and have them try to move in and take over while she was gone.

"I reckon I got two choices," she said to herself as she sat looking toward the trail that led to Denver.

"I can ride inta Denver, sell the burro and camp equipment ta some gold seeker, then find ah bank and sell enough gold so's I can catch a train ta Knoxville. Noble can ride in one of them stock cars. That way, when I get ta Knoxville, I can ride him home."

That was choice number one. Number two, she figured, was to head south down into Texas and maybe go see the Texas Ranger, Clay Brentwood, she'd met earlier. After all, he had invited her ta come see his spread.

The problem with the second choice was, it was out of her way, plus, she didn't know if he'd even be there, him out rangering so much of the time.

Once again, she remembered something her pappy had said. "Gal, if'n ya'll has mor'n one choice ta make, go with the one yer gut tells ya ta go with."

Well, that settled it; she thought to herself, she would go ta Denver, then on ta Knoxville and finally, home. It would take close ta two weeks to get there, and she figured the sooner she got back, the quicker she could start rebuilding and making sure those Mullins didn't try anything.

"Asides, once I get the place like I want it, I can hire somebody ta watch it whilest I go see what that good lookin' ranger has done ta rebuild his place," Loralie said to herself.

"Course, it would jest be ah friendly visit. Don't plan ta wind up livin' out in the middle o' nowheres, thout no mountains or trees."

Loralie shook her head, ashamed of herself for the thoughts she was thinking. She hardly knew the man.

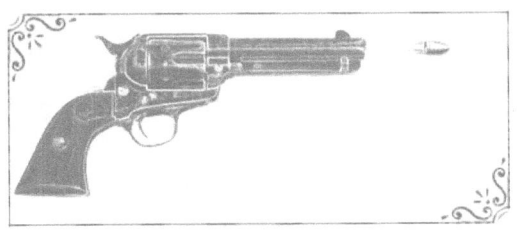

CHAPTER TWO

-

Clay Brentwood was restless. Lying around with nothing to do but read and eat had been okay for a couple of days, but three weeks was now grinding on his nerves. The wounds in his legs had healed and he wanted to get on with his life. He couldn't remember ever lying around this long, before.

Shortly after being shot by Clyde Millsap for busting up their attempted bank robbery in Fort Smith, Arkansas, his boss, Bill McDaniel, head of the Texas Rangers had come all the way from Austin to check on him and tell him he could take some time off.

Several weeks back, before Clay had left Austin, McDaniel had told him if he captured or killed Aaron Hammershield, he would speak to the judge about dropping, or at least reducing, Clay's two-year sentence to one of time served.

Unfortunately, the judge had had a heart attack and died, and the new judge would not change the former judge's decision.

So, what McDaniel came up with on his own was, for Clay to go on sick leave until he was needed again. This would allow him the freedom to go home and start rebuilding his ranch, with his promise to keep himself available for ranger work for the rest of his two-year sentence. And if he wasn't needed during that time, well, technically he would have served his time.

"Rangers don't have sick leave, so I'm makin' this decision on my own," McDaniel told him. "I know it's gonna take some time for your wounds ta heal and as far as I'm concerned, you've done everthing that was asked of you, but I can't release you from your sentence without a judge signin' off on it and this is the best I can come up with. What'ya say? You'll come if I need ya?"

Clay gladly agreed to the deal. He was tired of the fighting and killing, even though for the most part, the men he'd killed needed killing as far as he was concerned. Plus, he didn't want or need any more bullet scars, knife scars or any other kind of scars. He already had more than his share.

McDaniel settled up with him financially, then headed on back down to Austin. Some renegade Indians were causing trouble down around Hico, Texas and he needed to send a couple of men down to get it cleared up.

That had been three weeks ago. Today, after a lot of complaining, the doctor finally said, "Alright. You can go home or wherever you want to go. I've never seen a man so anxious to go back to dodging bullets."

The doctor was somewhat pacified when Clay explained he would be giving up chasing bad men for a while and would be going home to rebuild his ranch. After paying his bill, Clay shook hands with the doctor and thanked him for all he'd done, then headed for the sheriff's office to say his farewells to the man, who over the past three weeks, had become a friend.

The sheriff had also come close to dying during the shootout. He'd taken a bullet in his right arm that had been meant for his chest. The bullet had not only punctured a big hole in the sheriff's right arm, but also lodged itself in the bone, which had to be broken to remove the thirty-caliber slug.

He had healed nicely and had bullied the doctor into allowing him to go back to work within a week after being shot. His arm was bound tightly to hold the bone in place and he had to keep his arm in a sling. It was useless until it healed, but since he was left handed, he could still do paperwork. He'd even raised his hand and promised to let his deputies do all of the hard work. The doctor was like some ole mother hen when it came to his patients. The only reason the sheriff went back to the doctor's office was to let him check his arm, and to visit with Clay.

Clay and the sheriff were at the saloon having a farewell drink, when one of the sheriff's deputies came charging through the bat wing doors.

"Better come quick, Sheriff. Three men robbed the bank and taken two women hostage. Said they'd leave'm five miles out of town if nobody was chasin'm."

The sheriff looked at Clay then shook his head as he turned to the deputy. "How long have they been gone?"

"Only ah few minutes. No longer than it took me ta get here," the young man said.

Clay studied the young deputy and decided he was still a long way from being a lawman, but realized deputies weren't easy to find. At least this one seemed eager to learn.

The sheriff turned and looked at Clay, then stuck out his hand. "Hate ta cut this short, but I got some bank robbers ta try n' catch and ah couple of scared women who want ta get back home safe."

Clay sat his glass on the bar, reached into his vest pocket and pulled out his badge. He showed it to the sheriff, and said, "I'm still a ranger and my boss said I should come back inta service on an 'as needed' basis and we're wastin' time standin' here jawin'."

Fifteen minutes later, the sheriff, Clay and two deputies, who rode in a buckboard wagon, were headed south out of town. The trail was easy to follow. One of the horses had a loose shoe and left a trail a tenderfoot could follow.

The black stallion was glad to be out of his three-week confinement and strained to be let loose to run, but Clay held him to a gentle lope, knowing he might need the stallion's strength later on if there was a chase.

Five miles south of town they saw two women standing in the middle of the road, and as they approached, the women began jumping up and down, waving their arms.

After a brief questioning, they learned the three men had talked about going to Dallas, along with calling each other by names Clay thought he'd heard or read somewhere.

After the two deputies helped the ladies into the buckboard, they headed back toward Fort Smith.

Clay told the sheriff he doubted if the outlaws were going to Dallas. He figured they said that to throw them off the trail.

"Then where do you suppose they're headed? Did you recognize any of the names the ladies mentioned?" the sheriff asked.

Clay thought for a minute then said, "Actually, I do. I'm not sure, but I think I read some wanted posters with those names on'm, back in Austin."

"Will you be goin' after them, then?" the sheriff asked.

Clay got a puzzled look on his face. "What? You givin' up the chase already?"

The sheriff looked off toward the horizon. "Don't have any choice. My jurisdiction ran out when I left the town limits. It would only be legal if I had'm in site, which I don't."

Clay nodded his head. "Sorry ta lose ya, but I reckon I'll go on by myself."

Clay laid a rein on the stallion's neck and as the big horse turned, the sheriff said, "Now just you hold on ah gall-durned minute. I cain't let you go after'm all by yerself.

"Jurisdiction or no jurisdiction, it happened in my town and it was my bank that got robbed. I'm goin' along, badge er no badge."

Clay reined back toward the sheriff. "Sorry, sheriff, but I can't be responsible for any civilians."

"Then make me ah deputy," the sheriff said. "I ain't gonna let you go alone."

"What about your arm?" Clay asked seriously.

The sheriff pulled it out of the sling and shook it. "My arm's fine; just been usin' the sling as an excuse ta get outta certain chores."

That evening, Clay and his new deputy camped along a small stream where Clay caught three nice catfish, and was cooking them for dinner.

"You said you thought you'd heard their names before. Ain't that what you said?" the sheriff asked as he sipped on his coffee.

Clay turned the fish over, then looked over his shoulder at the sheriff. "There was ah Joseph Allen, along with Gus Bobbitt and ah D. B. Burrel, who are said ta be runnin' together in these parts. All wanted for bank robbin', horse thievin' and murder, as I recall."

"Jesus, I've heard of'm. Young too. A nasty bunch, and all with itchy trigger fingers."

There was a short space of time when their talking ceased. Men in this part of the country clammed up when it came time to eat. They could jaw all they wanted after, but when it came time ta eat, that's what they concentrated on. Eating was a serious business.

Over coffee and smokes, the sheriff asked, "So, if they ain't goin' ta Dallas, where do you think they're headed?"

Clay blew a smoke ring, then said, "Ain't real sure, but I'm bettin' it ain't Dallas; maybe Little Rock, or on south ta Texarkana, or maybe further still, on down ta Shreveport."

"You think we can trail'm that far?" the sheriff asked as he poured more coffee into his cup.

"Hope we don't have to, but if they don't get that horseshoe fixed we can. And if they don't, you can bet that horse is gonna come up lame and slow'm down, for sure."

"What if they just get rid of it and get another horse?"

"I guess they could do that, which would be the smartest thing ta do, but it won't matter, there are other tracks ta follow. One of the horses has an X on the corner of all of its shoes. Probably put there by the blacksmith who made'm. Plus, ah few miles back they met up with a fourth rider."

The sheriff nodded his head in wonder. Who was this ranger? It seemed he could track a snake through water.

"All of'm are men and leave deep tracks, while the fourth one is light and leaves shallow tracks. The light one is ridin' a horse with small hooves. Might even be a woman."

The sheriff thought for a moment, then said, "I got ah poster awhile back that said a woman named Lottie Simmons was tryin' ta build herself ah name like Belle Starr. You suppose it might be her?"

Clay just shrugged his shoulders.

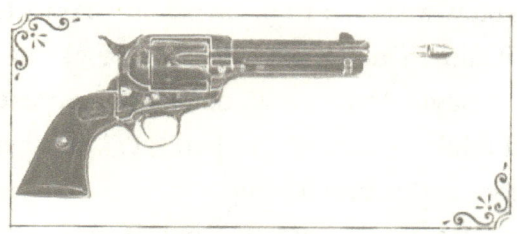

CHAPTER THREE

The train trip had been long and boring, nothing but miles and miles of the clickity clack sound of the rails. From time to time, Loralie saw small herds of buffalo, or antelope, which were something to see, but other than that, eastern Colorado and Kansas was nothing but flat land, and sometimes the wind rocked the cars so hard she thought the train would derail.

She had a layover in Wichita where she had to change trains and spend the night. The conductor told her the railroad would see to her horse. The next train would leave at nine in the morning.

After getting a room at the Heritage House, which boasted of soft beds, hot baths and the best food this side of heaven, Loralie realized she was getting stares because she was still dressed in buckskins. Even the man at the hotel was reluctant to rent her a room until she forked over cash. After putting her canvas bag in her room, she went to the hotel laundry.

The Chinaman who owned the place told her he couldn't clean her buckskins, but would be happy to dispose of them for her.

She had to admit they were startin' ta get ah mite ripe and could probably stand in the corner all by themselves. And after only three years of wearin', too, but she hated to throw them away.

Two blocks from the hotel, she found what she was looking for, a women's clothing store. Thirty minutes later she was in her room taking a hot bath; the first real one she'd had in more than a year.

After toweling off, she put on the dress she'd purchased. It was the first dress she'd ever owned. She twirled round and round, liking the freedom not felt dressed in the buckskins. The dress fit her like a glove and showed off her womanly figure. It was a soft, white material, with red roses and a full skirt. She looked at herself in the full-length mirror and said, "Loralie Benson, you do fill out ah woman's dress right nicely."

It took her another thirty minutes of fussing with her hair before she decided it looked all right. Her hair had never been all that important before, but with her new clothes… and smelling all fresh and clean…

Last came her shoes. She'd never owned a pair of women's shoes before. She'd always worn homemade moccasins or hand me down boots from her brothers.

They felt strange and tight, and she wasn't sure she could walk in them. The heels were a site higher than the boots she'd worn. She walked around her room for a good ten minutes to get the feel of them. She didn't leave her room until she felt she could walk without falling down and making a fool of herself.

For the first time in her twenty-three years, she felt like a lady. Oh, she didn't have the book learning they did and she couldn't talk sweet and proper, but what she saw in the mirror, made her feel good. She would have danced, if she knew any other kind except the kind they did at the barn dances back in the hills.

When she came down the stairs and walked into the lobby, the man behind the desk took a double take to make sure it was the same woman he'd rented a room to. This one was beautiful and it seemed to him the roses on her dress matched her red hair. He averted his eyes before his wife caught him staring.

As Loralie walked toward the restaurant, men smiled and tipped their hats. She smiled and nodded her head slightly, afraid to say anything that would give her away for the mountain girl she was.

In the doorway of the restaurant, Loralie stood for a moment, trying to catch her breath. She'd never been in a room this elegant. Red velvet upholstery with gold trim seemed to fill the room. All the tables had white tablecloths, and real silverware. There were real glasses sitting next to the white cloth napkins, and overhead were giant chandeliers that had at least a hundred candles on each one. She'd seen pictures of rooms like this in books, but never expected to actually eat in such an elegant place.

An elderly man, dressed in black pants and a white shirt, escorted her to her table and asked if anyone would be joining her?

She blushed and said; "No, I'm alone," in her best proper English, knowing there was still a bit of Tennessee twang to her voice.

The man smiled and said, "I understand. First time in Wichita?" he asked.

Loralie smiled and nodded her head.

"If I may take the liberty, I would like to help you with your dinner choices."

"Yes, thank you. And if I could, I'd like to have somethin' special like," she said, starting to feel relaxed around this man.

"I believe I have the perfect choice," he said with a smile. "And by the way, I was born and raised in Nashville, but that will be our little secret. And you may call me, Henry."

Loralie reached out and touched his arm. "Thank you, Henry. And I'm good at keeping secrets."

Henry smiled and took a pad and pencil from his shirt pocket. "And now, may I suggest something from the French menu?"

"Oh yes," Loralie giggled. "I've never had fancy food afore and French is about as fancy as ah person can get."

Henry smiled as he wrote on his pad, "We'll start with Coquilles St-Jaques."

When Loralie looked at him like he had a third eye, Henry smiled and said, "That would be gratineed scallops, madam."

Loralie nodded her head slightly and said, "Of course it is," still with no idea what that was.

The rest of her meal consisted of a winter salad with buttermilk dressing, followed by Blanquette de Veau, which turned out to be veal covered with cream sauce. Loralie had never eaten veal before and found she liked it.

And for dessert, she had chocolate mousse. When Henry served the dessert, he held out a block of chocolate and grated pieces onto the top.

Loralie thought she'd died and gone to heaven.

And of course, with the scallops, there had been white wine, and with the veal, red wine. It wasn't as strong as the moonshine back home, but for some reason it made her feel a bit giddy and lightheaded. She'd never drank wine before.

By the time she finished, she felt like a princess. Henry had been very attentive. "So, this is how the rich folks eat?" she asked of Henry when she finished and wiped her mouth with the very first real napkin she'd ever used. "Sure beats beans and fatback."

Henry nodded and said, "I'm happy madam is pleased."

She made sure Henry received a large tip for all his help and making her feel like a lady instead of a country bumpkin.

She knew she was splurging her money, but what the heck; she deserved a reward for all her hard work in the cold rivers of Colorado. Besides, what little she'd spent wasn't a drop in the bucket compared ta what was left.

When the train pulled out of Wichita, headed for Little Rock, Arkansas, Loralie looked out of the window and saw Henry standing on the platform and she waved at him. Henry lifted his homburg and bowed at the hips.

At that point, something happened inside her and she knew she'd never felt more like a lady than she did right now. She leaned back in her seat and made a vow to learn more about reading, writing and doing ciphers. She would try hard to become ah lady. "Ya don't need ta be ah tomboy ta run ah horse or cattle spread," she said to herself. "Sides, I'll be lockin' horns with male buyers who think they can best me jest cause I'm ah female. Well, that ain't gonna happen. I'll show'm, no matter what."

Loralie sat daydreaming about how she would rebuild her home on Cinch Mountain. Her pa would have scoffed at her decisions but she didn't care. There would not be ah log cabin this time. She would build a big white house, like she'd seen pictures of; with ah barn painted red. And she would have nice furniture inside her house. She leaned back in her seat and dreamed about her future, wondering if the Texas Ranger, Clay Brentwood, would approve.

She was gazing out of the window when two men came riding out of a ditch and raced alongside the train. The one closest to the train jumped from his horse onto the landing of the car she was in.

Without thinking twice, Loralie shoved her satchel under her seat and hefted her newly purchased ladies bag onto her lap.

She had bought one big enough to hold her thirty-two-caliber pistol, along with some ladies niceties, and sack of licorice.

The door at the end of the car opened and a man with a bandana tied just below his eyes stepped in, holding a pistol in his hand.

Loralie reached into her handbag and took hold of her own pistol.

"Ever'body just stay calm and nobody will die," the bandit said waving his pistol. Looking down at the man sitting in the first seat, he handed him a saddlebag and said, "Put your money and valuables in the bag, then pass it back."

As each person did as he or she was told, the bandit watched to make sure they didn't miss anything.

When he got to Loralie, his eyes lit up and he touched his fingers to the brim of his hat. "Ah purty lady like you might cause a fella ta give up the owl hoot trail, but I guess you wouldn't go fer ah man like me," he said, and when she said nothing, he sighed and said, his eyes turning cold and hard. "Yer jewels and yer money."

Loralie smiled her sweetest smile and watched his reaction, which gave her the time she needed. She pulled her hand out of the bag; but instead of money or jewels, she was holding her pistol and before the outlaw could react, she shot him in the arm holding his pistol, then lowered her pistol and shot him in the knee.

The man dropped his pistol and fell to the floor of the coach, screaming like a small child, "You shot me! Damn you woman, you shot me!"

She picked up the saddlebags and tossed them to the man across the aisle. "See that ever'body gets their valuables back," then looked down at the outlaw.

"Well ain't you jest ah wonderment. First, ya compliment me, then you turn around and yell at me. If they don't hang ya, maybe you should try ta find some other kind of work."

By then, the few men who were armed were shooting out of the window at the second outlaw, and as he rode away, a bullet caught him in the back of the head. The last anyone saw of him was when he was pitched head first off his horse.

One of the men on the train was a veterinarian, and after removing the bullets Loralie put into the man's hand and knee, he said, "I guess you'll live to stand trial."

Suddenly, Loralie was inundated with thank yous from the other passengers.

She smiled and said, "I was jest pertectin' what's mine, which ain't much, but it's all I got. Y'all jest happened ta get yer stuff saved too."

After they'd gone back to their seats, Loralie sighed. "This here becomin' ah lady ain't gonna be so easy as I thought," she said to herself. "But I sure weren't gonna let him have my gold. I worked too hard ta get it and I jest ain't gonna hand it over to the first owl hoot that points ah gun at me. He wants gold, let him go hunt fer it like I did."

The man's hands were tied behind his back, and he was sitting in a vacant seat, being watched by one of the men passengers until they could get to the next town where he would be turned over to the local sheriff.

CHAPTER FOUR

Between the tracks he was following and his gut feeling, Clay ruled out Texarkana as a town they would run to, not enough excitement there. If this Lottie, whatever her name was, was leading this gang, she would want ta go where there was bright lights and gambling, especially if she was trying to imitate Belle Starr. Texarkana didn't seem to be a likely place. It was too small. She would head for Little Rock, and from there maybe on over to Memphis, which was just a hop, skip and a jump from Little Rock - not more than two and a half to three days on horseback, and not that long if they took the train. Memphis was full of vice; and like a magnet, it would draw her there.

Bill Hancock thought Clay's thinking had logic as they headed southeast along the Arkansas River, the most likely route the outlaws might have taken.

A couple of hours later, Clay pulled the black stallion to a halt and stepped down. The tracks were there, clear as a sunny sky. The small horse looked to be in the lead and the one with the

X marked on the hooves was next. The other two were not far behind. The horse with the loose shoe was beginning to limp. It wouldn't be long before its rider would have to do something; either fix the shoe or get another horse.

Three hours later, close to the river and just inside a small grove of elm and walnut trees, Clay and Bill were setting up a campsite for the night and putting water on to boil for coffee when they heard a single shot from farther down the river, maybe a mile or so.

"That sounded like a pistol shot to me, although at that distance it's hard ta tell the difference," Sheriff Hancock said, looking in the direction the sound came from.

"Maybe the man's horse finally gave up," Clay said shaking his head. "Damn shame how some people treat their animals."

The sheriff nodded in agreement as he sliced up a potato and an onion and dumped it all into the skillet of hot bacon grease. Morning would be soon enough to check it out. The sun was already dipping behind the trees and hunting outlaws in the dark was a sure way to get yourself killed.

The next morning, they rode up and stopped next to a horse that was limping around, feeding on the lush green grass near the river.

Not far away, they saw the body of one of the outlaws lying face down in the dirt. He'd been shot in the back and left there for the animals to feed on.

"Well, I guess that makes one less outlaw ta run down," Clay said, looking around for some place to bury the man. "The man might be an outlaw but he deserves ah proper buryin', instead of left layin' out here for the wolves ta eat," he said to the sheriff, who nodded his head in agreement.

They didn't have a shovel but found a gully where they dragged his body into and piled rocks over him. When they finished, Clay took off his hat and said, "Lord, I ain't much on prayin', so I reckon I'm just gonna leave it up to your judgment as what ta do with this man. He was an outlaw, but maybe he had some good in him. He looks too young ta have done too much bad."

Before they left, Clay walked over and repaired the horse's shoe with a file and nails he carried in his saddlebags in case his own horse threw a shoe.

When he finished, he loosened the cinch some, then dropped a lead rope over his head and mounted the black stallion.

"Think he'll be okay?" Hancock asked.

"Oh sure. Now that the shoe is fixed he'll be his old self again in no time. We'll take it easy for a few miles."

The day turned out to be a scorcher and the ground they covered was rough, but the tracks were still easy to follow. By the time the sun was creeping below the far horizon, they were tired and hungry. The horses were in no better shape and Clay had just decided to call it a day when Hancock noticed a whiff of smoke lifting into the sky, not half a mile ahead.

"What'a ya make of that?" he asked, pointing in the direction of the smoke.

Clay looked at it for a moment, then turned to the sheriff. "Guess we should make some coffee and give the horses a little rest. Looks like we've got some night work ta do."

It was around two in the morning when Clay and the sheriff stepped down from their horses and eased up to the top of the small rise and looked down on the outlaw camp.

The fire was not much more than embers. In the moonlight they saw three people rolled up in their blankets. One of them was off a short distance from the other two.

"Probably the woman," Clay whispered.

Hancock nodded his head in agreement. "What's the plan?" he asked, leaving the final decision to Clay.

Clay studied the area. The river was on one side, which would make that escape route a mite difficult. Trees surrounded the rest of the campsite, also making escape, not impossible, but not too easy, either.

"You ease down on this side 'til you get close, but not close enough to spook their horses. I'll circle around and come in from the other side. That way they might think they're surrounded, which they will be, sorta," Clay whispered.

"When you see me step into the clearing, you come ah runnin', yellin' at the top of your lungs and I'll do the same. Should scare'm enough to give us the time we need ta get the drop on'm," Clay said moving back toward the horses to get his moccasins.

When Clay disappeared into the forest, Hancock pulled his pistol from his holster and checked the cylinder to make sure it was loaded with six rounds, then laid down on his belly and began to crawl toward their camp. He took his time, removing anything that might make a noise, allowing time for Clay to get to the other side of their camp.

When the sheriff got as close as he dared without spooking their horses, he waited and watched for the ranger to come out of the trees on the far side of the clearing.

It took Clay nearly thirty minutes to make his way around the camp and get close. They were all still sleeping soundly as was indicated by the snoring comin' from the two men. Clay tried to see the woman, but the trees sheltered her and he couldn't quite make her out from this direction.

Clay took a deep breath, then ran into the clearing, yelling and shooting his pistol in the air. "Texas Rangers! You're surrounded! Show yourselves with your hands reachin' for the sky, or grab for iron and die where you lay."

Bill Hancock ran in from the opposite side of the camp and pointed his pistol at the two men on the ground who were sitting up, wild eyed and holding their hands above their heads.

Clay noticed the woman hadn't moved and ran over and touched her with his toe. "You need ta get up lady. We ain't wantin' ta hurt ya, but the choice will be yours," he said, keeping a wary eye in case she came up shooting."

When she didn't move, Clay, pistol in one hand and a stick in the other, pulled the blanket back, revealing some tree limbs and brush. Just then he heard a female voice yell and the sound of several horses running away.

"Ah hell," he said as he ran in the direction of the fleeing horses, knowing he had made a stupid mistake by not checking them before charging into their camp.

In the moonlight, he saw a rider riding hard to the south before she disappeared around a bend in the river, followed by two panic-stricken horses.

After tying up the two outlaws, Clay turned to the sheriff and said, "I'll go round up their horses and bring'm back."

"What then?" the sheriff asked.

"Somebody needs ta take these two back ta town and I reckon that should be you."

"And you'll be goin' after the other one," Sheriff Hancock said, nodding his head as he turned and looked at the two young men. "Was the one that took off and left you ta hang out ta dry, a woman by the name of Lottie Simmons?"

One of the outlaws, a young man with a crooked nose and one crossed eye, who called himself, Gus Bobbitt, said, "It was all her doin'. We only went along 'cause she made certain promises, if you know what I mean."

"Who shot your friend? The one with the horse that was limping?" the sheriff asked.

The second outlaw, also a young man who was barely growing peach fuzz on his face, spoke up, "When Joe complained, Joseph Allen, that was his name, well when he said we needed to slow down until he could get another horse, she pulled her pistol and shot him in the back. Then she looked at me and said, D. B., if you and Gus can't keep up you'll wind up just like him. She might be mighty good on the eyes but she's ah mean, evil woman."

After getting a complete description of Lottie, Clay stepped aboard the black stallion and headed down the river at a fast pace. After no more than half a mile, he found the two horses grazing quietly.

He took the horses back and told the sheriff he'd send a telegram as soon as he had her in custody. With that, he nudged the black stallion with the sides of his boots and headed south, again. The full moon helped Clay follow the tracks, which led to the road that went to Little Rock. There her tracks mingled with the other horse and wagon tracks, but by now Clay didn't really need to see a trail. She was headed for Little Rock, a town where she might have ah place to hide, or catch a train to Memphis.

The black stallion was feeling good and Clay allowed him to set his own pace.

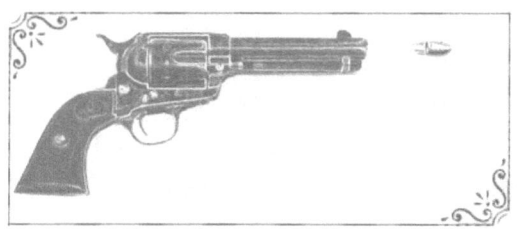

CHAPTER FIVE

The Arkansas River was the site of many townships, including Little Rock, so named because of a large rock sitting at the edge of the river.

The town was growing by leaps and bounds. There must be more than twenty thousand people, Clay guessed as he rode through town.

At the north end of town, he found what he was looking for. If Lottie was here, this is where he would find her.

The third saloon he went into, he saw a familiar face. A few years back, the bartender had worked as the head bartender at the Deleno House up in Wichita, where they had met and had become friends.

"Hello, Walt," Clay said as he stepped up to the bar. You're ah far piece from home, ain'tcha?"

The tall, skinny bartender turned at the sound of his name, a grin breaking across his face. "Well if this don't beat all. Heard you got hitched and took up ranchin' down in Texas. What in the world are you doing here?"

Clay was about to respond when Walt saw the ranger badge pinned on Clay's shirt and pointed, "Your ah Texas Ranger, now I see. Man, we've got some catching up to do. Let me get you a beer, then you can bring me up to date."

Walt poured one for himself, then told the other bartender he would be taking a break.

At a corner table, Clay told Walt the whole story, and when he finished, Walt leaned back in his chair and whistled. "Man alive, you've been down the road and across the river. Are you alright?"

Clay nodded his head in the affirmative and asked, "What about you?" wanting to change the subject.

Walt grinned one of those sheepish grins and said, "Same ole story, I met this woman and the first thing you know, I'm smitten. Followed her here from Wichita. She had an aunt that lived here and passed on, leaving her a house and some money and with what I had put by, we bought this place."

"None of my business," Clay said, "but was she ah workin' girl before you met her?"

Walt slapped his hand down on the table and said, "That's the thing," Walt said. "She'd never been inside a saloon before she met me. And here's the rub, she's a preacher's daughter who was looking for a way out and along I came."

"Ah preacher's daughter? Now don't that beat all? And are things workin' out for ya?"

Before Walt could respond, a very pretty woman in her early thirties walked up and smiled down at them. She was dressed in a light gray dress trimmed in auburn red. Her coal black hair hung loose down around her shoulders, and she had the deepest blue eyes Clay had ever seen.

Clay stood up and took off his hat.

Walt stood up and took her hand. "Clay, this is my wife, Cynthia," then turned to his wife and said, "Honey, this is Clay Brentwood from Wichita. He's a Texas Ranger now."

Clay shook her hand and said, "It's my pleasure, Mrs. Pullman. Will you join us?"

"Thank you," she said as she sat down. "Walt has spoken of you many times."

The other bartender brought them another round and a glass of wine for her.

By the way they looked at each other, Clay could tell they had a good marriage.

After a few minutes of chitchat, Clay got down to business and asked about Lottie.

Cynthia put her hand on Walt's shoulder and his face turned blood red. "Oh yes, Miss Lottie Simmons came by yesterday looking for a place to stay for a few days. She offered Walt pleasures beyond his wildest dreams if he would let her have a room, didn't she, honey?" Cynthia said, poking Walt in the ribs with her elbow. "Poor Walt just stood there with his jaw hanging down to his chest, his face as red as a turnip. But I sent her packing, didn't I, darling?"

Walt nodded his head and took a drink of beer.

Clay couldn't help himself and burst out laughing, and in a few seconds, they were all laughing. Finally, when Clay calmed down, he asked, "You wouldn't happen to know where she went, would you?"

"Don't know where she spent the night, but she caught the morning train for Memphis. I just happened to be down there sending a telegram, ordering some whiskey, when she came in. Gave me the high nose," Walt said with a grin.

"She's running from the law, isn't she?" Cynthia asked.

"Yes ma'am. She and some would be outlaws robbed a bank back in Fort Smith, then she shot one of her own gang because his horse threw a shoe and slowed'm down. We caught the rest of her gang and now I plan on arrestin' her and takin' her and the money back to Fort Smith.

Walt whistled, "You just never know, do you?"

Since the next train to Memphis didn't leave until sometime tomorrow because of rail repairs being made, Clay accepted their offer of a room and supper, then stood up and excused himself. He needed to see to his horse and headed for the door, not noticing the man sitting at a table near the back of the room who had been watching him ever since he'd entered.

Clay had just lifted the reins and was about to step into the stirrup when the man from the back table walked out and yelled, "Hey, you! Get your hands off that horse!"

Clay turned and looked at the man and what he saw was trouble in capital letters. The man was dressed in black except for a red bandana around his neck. The man wore a brace of pearl handled pistols, tied down low in the gunfighter style. His feet were slightly spread and his hands hung down, close to the butts of his pistols.

"And why should I do that?" Clay asked.

"Because that horse belongs to a friend of mine. You stole it from her two days ago, and she barely got away with her life."

By now, Walt and his wife had come out of the saloon and stood a short distance away. Several other people had stopped when the gunfighter yelled at Clay.

In a loud voice, Walt said, "You'd best back off, mister. I know this man and can vouch that he is no horse thief."

It was as if Walt had never said anything. The gunfighter stared at Clay and said, "I'm calling you a horse thief. What are you going to do about it?"

For just a moment, Clay stood there, wondering what action to take, then looked at the gunfighter and asked, "The woman's name wouldn't happen to be Lottie Simmons, would it?"

"What if it is?" the gunfighter said. "Her name ain't got nothing to do with the fact that you stole her horse and tried to rape her, and I'm calling you on it."

Clay sighed, trying to think of a way out of havin' a shootout with this man, but nothing came to mind. The man was a professional killer and was hell bent on earning his pay.

Clay looked at the man, deciding to try one more time and said, "I've never stolen any horses, nor raped any women, in my entire life. You've been bamboozled by a pretty face and false promises. Just take the money she paid you and leave, and we'll forget this whole incident."

"You're a liar, and I'm callin' you," the gunfighter said, then yelled, "Draw!"

The man was fast, Clay had to admit that, but not fast enough. Clay's reaction had been instantaneous. The gunfighter's pistol had barely cleared leather when Clay's bullet dug a hole into the man's chest, right over his heart.

The gunfighter's eyes went wide in astonishment for just a moment before he toppled face first into the street.

The town marshal came running up with a shotgun in his right hand, just as Clay was holstering his pistol. "What's going on here?" he asked, pointing the shotgun in Clay's direction.

"The man accused me of stealin' this horse," Clay said, pointing in the direction of the black stallion. "I told him he was mistaken and he pulled on me. I had no choice but to defend myself."

The marshal was a man in his fifties and had fought in the war as a sergeant for the north. For the past ten years, he'd been marshal and thought of himself as a fair man. He looked at the people standing nearby and each one of them nodded their head in agreement of what Clay had said.

Walt stepped off the porch and explained the whole thing to the marshal and when he finished, the marshal looked at Clay and asked, "That true? You're a Texas Ranger in pursuit of the woman who hired this gun slick to kill you?"

Clay nodded his head. "That's about the size of it, Marshal." Clay reached into his pocket and pulled out ten dollars and held the money toward the marshal. "This should cover his burial."

"You don't have to do that," the marshal said, taking the money.

"I know," Clay said, then turned to Walt. "I'll be takin' care of Midnight, then I'll be along."

Late into the night, Clay stared at the ceiling, wondering why his life had taken the turn it had. His dreams of havin' ah horse and cattle ranch, along with some sons one day had seemed to evaporate like steam off a cup of coffee.

Even when his boss had given him the opportunity to go home for a while, somehow, instead of goin' home like he'd planned, he'd wound up chasin' this Lottie Simmons, and killin' another man in a shootout.

The next morning, after breakfast, Clay sent a telegram to his boss in Austin, explaining where he was and that he was planning on going to Memphis.

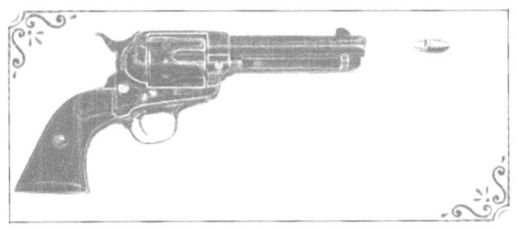

CHAPTER SIX

Loralie stepped off the train in Little Rock, Arkansas and looked around. It was balmy and the sun was scorching hot. She had decided to take the southern route, through Little Rock, then over to Memphis, and from there to Knoxville. She stood letting her eyes take in the growing town and was not impressed. In the far distance, she saw a man riding a black horse and for just a moment she was about to call out, but a cloud of dark train smoke filled the area and when it cleared, the man was no longer in sight.

It couldn't be Clay Brentwood, she thought to herself. What would he be doin' in Little Rock? That would be a long way out of his territory, but still, her eyes searched the street as she walked her horse in the direction of the livery stable.

She had a layover because of work being done on the tracks up ahead, somewhere. It seemed the train was almost as slow as riding a horse and by now she was getting tired of riding trains with nothing to do but stare out of the window or read a book, which she had been doing. In Wichita, she'd picked up a copy of a book called, David Copperfield. She'd heard about the author, Charles Dickens. The book had kept her glued to her seat, but by the time they reached Little Rock, she had finished it and was hoping she could find something else to read before the train left for Memphis.

After seeing to the big Morgan, she headed for the hotel just down the street and as she stepped onto the step leading to the lobby of the hotel, a man grabbed her by the arm.

Loralie jerked her arm loose and looked up at a giant of a man dressed in patched, filthy buckskins. The man stunk somethin' awful and looked as though he hadn't had ah bath in weeks, or even longer, and the scorching heat didn't make him smell any better.

"Hold on there, lil lady. I got money and I can pay. Ain't been with ah woman in more'n six months and I'm ah hankerin' after you."

Loralie smoothed the front of her dress, trying to decide how to deal with this man. Finally, she said, "I'm sorry, sir, but I think you have me confused with someone else. I'm not ah workin' girl."

"Don't care if'n you are or not. You're the one I got my eye on and you're the one I'm gonna have." And with that he reached out and grabbed her again, and began to drag her down the street.

Loralie was kicking and screaming, but she couldn't break loose from his powerful grip.

"You can kick and scream all you want, lil lady, but I'm takin' you out ta my camp down by the river and you and me, we's gonna have us some fun."

People stood, frozen, watching, but no one offered her any help. "What's the matter with you people?" she yelled. "Can't you see I need help? This animal is gonna rape me and you jest stand there, ah gawkin'!"

"No use you ah hollerin' and such. Ain't nobody gonna help you. I'm big Jack Baldwin and I've done whooped most of the would be tough men in this here town. Ain't nobody wants ta tangle with me, includin' the law."

"Let her go," a cold, hard voice said.

Jack stopped and turned around, still holding Loralie's arm in a steel grip. He looked up at a man sitting on a black horse and took the man's measure. He looked ta be a man who could handle himself, and the pistol on his hip was tied down in the gunfighter style. But it was the Texas Ranger badge that intrigued him. Jack liked whippin' lawmen.

"You one of them Texas Rangers I've heered bout?"

Loralie couldn't believe her eyes. It had been him she'd seen earlier and now, he just appeared out of nowhere like some knight in shining armor. Well, he didn't really have on any armor, but here he was, coming to her aid, again.

Clay looked down at Loralie and said, "You sure do find ah way ta get yourself inta trouble ever time I'm around, don't'cha."

Her heart was beating so loud she thought he could hear. "Howdy Clay," she said. "Sure seems that way don't it? I sure am glad ta see ya, though. I was mindin' my own business when this brute grabbed me and said he was takin' me ta his camp, tellin' me what he intended ta do once we got out there, and I reckon I don't hav'ta tell ya, I was ah mite scared."

Clay stepped down from his horse and dropped the reins to the ground. "I said, let her go, and I won't say it again," he said walking up to the mountain of a man.

Jack Baldwin looked down at the man and saw something in his eyes that told him he couldn't run roughshod over him. But that was the very thing that excited him. Most men cowered in his presence, but not this one. Jack hoped the fight would last more than a couple of minutes.

"Sure, sure, anythin' fer ah Texas Ranger," he said as he gave Loralie a shove away from him.

Clay looked at the man and knew this wasn't the end of it. There were too many people standing nearby and the man would lose face if he let a smaller man tell him what to do.

Jack stepped in and threw a roundhouse punch, intending to end it with just one blow, but Clay had expected it and stepped under the swing and drove a left fist into Jack's midsection with everything he had.

Jack felt the wind being knocked out of him and stepped back to catch his breath, but the ranger followed him and drove a right to his kidney.

This was not the way he'd envisioned it. He reached out and grabbed the ranger by the arm and jerked him in close, then wrapped his tree trunk arms around him and began to squeeze. No man had ever broken his grip before and he grinned at the thought of besting this ranger in front of the townsfolk standin' nearby.

Clay knew he had to get loose. The man was strong and would break his back if he didn't do something, quick. He pulled his arms in between him and the big man, and pushed, releasing some of the pressure, then drove his knee into the big man's crotch.

Jack yelled and let go. He stepped away from Clay, trying to get his breath back and let the pain in his groin ease up some.

Jack Baldwin was as mad as an agitated bumblebee. He was being whipped by a man half his size and in front of the townsfolk, and that just wouldn't do.

Taking a deep breath, Jack waded back in and caught Clay with a left hook that lifted him off his feet.

Clay hit the street on his back and saw bright lights going on and off in his head. Getting to his feet he knew he had to keep away from punches like that, he couldn't take many more and still stay on his feet.

More wary now, Clay danced around, looking for his chance. He feigned a left and when the big man dodged, Clay hit him square on the nose with a straight right. Blood gushed from Jack's nose and ran down into his beard.

This stopped Jack only long enough for him to wipe his nose. He roared and drove himself at Clay with his arms out wide.

The man was bent over and the only thing Clay could do was to drop down low and turn so the man ran into his backside. With his left hand, Clay grabbed Jack by the belt and with his right; he grabbed a handful of beard and pulled hard.

Jack's weight coming forward helped Clay to lift and throw the big man over his shoulder.

Jack landed flat of his back and felt the air being driven from him. Pain radiated throughout his whole body, and for just an instant, Jack wasn't sure he could get up. Then something inside him came alive and wouldn't let this little man best him and he heaved himself up.

Clay was waiting for him and drove his right fist into Jack's midsection, again, trying to end the fight once and for all.

Instead, the mountain of a man took the blow and kept coming. Clay felt the man's ham like fist drive itself into his ribs. Pain roared through his side and suddenly he had a hard time breathing. Before he could react, Jack hit him square in the face. Lights went off and on in Clay's head and he felt his eyes begin to swell and he had a hard time seeing. He did the only thing he could think of to do. He ran head first at Jack and rammed him in the stomach, causing them both to go down.

When they finally got to their feet, both men were panting hard. The big man's left eye was swollen shut and his broken nose was still bleeding, but he wasn't done for yet. With strength that only a man of his size could have, he hit Clay alongside the head.

Clay went airborne and saw the street coming up to meet him and knew the pain he was going to feel from his injured ribs when he hit the ground. He pulled his left arm against his side and stuck out his right arm to help break the fall. It helped a little, but even so, he almost passed out. The only thing that kept him awake was the thought of what the man would do to him if he blacked out.

He hit the street rolling and came to his feet. Holding his left arm against his side, he turned to face the big man and said, "That all you got, you big tub ah guts?" knowing this would enrage the big man and hopefully cause him to do something stupid.

Jack's eyes were filled with hate and he charged Clay, arms spread wide. Clay waited until the last moment, then stepped aside and kicked Jack in the knee, knocking him off balance. His weight sent him headfirst into a large wagon sitting nearby.

Because of his condition, his size and weight, Jack couldn't stop himself from ramming into the wagon headfirst. The people standing nearby heard the sound of Jack's neck snapping as it hit the side of the wagon.

People gathered around and looked down at the man who had been bullying them for weeks. He lay face up, but his neck and head was at a crooked angle.

Lawrence Whitehead, the local doctor, stepped off the sidewalk and knelt down and checked Jack's neck, then stood up.

"He's dead. Broke his neck when he hit the wagon. Go on about your business, I'll see he gets taken down to the mortician."

Clay limped up and looked down at the big man. "I wasn't aim'in on him bein' killed. I just couldn't let him drag the lady off like that," he said, indicating Loralie.

Clay reached into his pocket and pulled out some money and said, "I'll pay the buryin' bill."

Before he could give the doctor any money, Loralie rushed up and said, "No you won't. I'll pay the bill. It was my honor you was pertectin'."

"You strike it rich up in Colorado, did ya?" Clay asked through swollen lips.

Loralie flinched, seeing him try to speak when he was obviously in a lot of pain. "Let's jest say I did what I went up there ta do and I want ta thank ya for what ya did, and I'm payin' fer you ta see ah doctor and there'll be no discussin' about it," Loralie said in a rapid-fire speech.

Doctor Whitehead stepped up and took Clay by the arm. "I'm a doctor and if you'll come to my office, I'll see to your wounds, which looks to be more than a few," then turned to Loralie and said, "And there will be no charge. Jack's horse, saddle and gear, plus whatever money he has on him, should be more than enough to cover everything."

After the doctor finished patching Clay up as best he could, Loralie helped him over to the hotel and got him a room. Once she got him to lie down, which wasn't easy, he kept telling her he had things to do and a train to catch, but she insisted he rest. He could catch another train later. Once he was asleep, she eased out of the room and took his horse down to the livery.

The holster greeted her. He had seen the fight and was eager to talk about it. "I sure would'a bet money that ranger wouldn't ah lasted no time atall against Jack. Glad I didn't bet nuthin'. And you can tell him there'll be no charge. That big galoot came in here and got several buckets of oats fer his horse and didn't pay fer nery ah one. Sos I reckon that ranger earned hisself ah free horse boardin'."

That evening, Loralie brought hot soup to Clay's room. His face was swollen and black and blue and his injured ribs still made it hard to breathe. He was in no condition to go out in public.

Clay's eyes were swollen almost all the way shut and he had to sip his soup through puffed lips.

Loralie sat in a chair across the room, staring at him. He looked like a herd of horses had trampled him. His face was black and blue and so swollen he could hardly see or talk. The doctor said his ribs weren't broken, but badly bruised, and would take a while to heal. He'd wrapped Clay's ribs and both hands in gauze and told him to soak his hands in brine water every day for a week, if he could.

She wanted to go to him and hold him and tell him how sorry she was. It was because of her he was in this condition, but that wouldn't be proper, nor, in his condition, could he stand to be hugged.

Clay finished the soup and thanked her, then said he should probably get some more rest. He was beginning to feel a mite uncomfortable with her in his room.

Loralie looked at him and said, "I'm real sorry this happened. Wouldn't blame ya if'n you rode shy if'n you ever see me again."

Clay winced as he tried to smile through his swollen lips. "Other than bein' pretty as a picture, it wasn't your fault. You just happened to be in the wrong place at the wrong time."

Loralie felt her face getting red and before she could respond, Clay went on.

"That sure is a pretty dress you have on; goes good with your hair and eyes."

"Now why'd ya hav'ta go and say somethin' like thet?" she said as tears formed in her eyes and she rushed from the room, not wanting him to see her cry. Her face was flushed and her heart was beating heavily. She couldn't allow herself ta fall in love with ah flatlander. She was ah mountain girl through and through.

Clay leaned back and allowed himself to smile just a little bit. She sure looked like a lady in that dress and pretty as a newborn colt.

He needed rest but he also needed information. He figured he would sleep for an hour or so, then slip out and ask if anyone knew anything else about Lottie. He hoped there would be no more of her gunmen looking for him. He wondered what he would do if there was? In his condition, they could probably whip him all up and down the street. Maybe Loralie would come to his rescue. With that thought, he fell asleep.

Clay awoke with a start and sat up in the bed, listening, but the only sound he heard was the tinny piano down at the saloon. With great effort, he pulled on his boots, put on his hat and strapped on his pistol - all without lighting the lamp sitting on a small table next to his bed.

Clay went out the back door of the hotel and stayed away from lighted areas as much as he could. Even at two o'clock in the morning, Little Rock was a busy place. Cards, liquor, women of the night, and other vices were available to anyone seeking pleasure. Because the town had become a center for several train lines, it was never without clients from both, passengers and railroad workers, along with cowboys and the locals.

Still in the shadow of the building, Clay pulled his hat down low to help cover his bruised face, then peeked in the front window of the nearest saloon, but saw no one whom he might ask questions.

After peeking into the windows of every saloon in town, and there were six of them, Clay was ready to call it a night. He was tired and his body ached from the top of his head to the tip of his toes.

As silently as he had come, he returned to the back door of the hotel and eased it open and was about to enter when a voice stopped him cold.

"Well, Mister Ranger man, did you have yerself ah good time?"

Loralie was standing just inside the back door with her arms folded across her chest.

Clay raised his finger to his lips indicating she be quiet, then motioned for her to follow him to his room.

Once inside, he lit the lamp, pulled down the shade and pointed toward the only chair in the room, a hardback wooden one that had seen better days.

When Loralie sat down, Clay eased himself down on the bed and took a minute to catch his breath. Before he had a chance to say anything, Loralie looked at him with fire in her eyes and said, "I went to ah lot of trouble ta get ah tub filled with hot water sos you could soak in it and when I come ta get ya, you're out on the town, doin' God only knows what."

Clay smiled. She was pretty even when she was madder than a wet hen.

"Do you honestly think I could go out drinkin' or tomcattin' in the condition I'm in? Maybe I gave you too much credit in the common sense department."

Loralie stood up and put her hands on her hips. "Well what was I supposed ta think? At this time of night that's about the only reason fer ah man ta be out."

By now, it was close to five in the morning and through a space at the side of the window shade, Clay could see the restaurant down the street was just opening up.

"Maybe, if you'll get down off your high horse and help me down to the restaurant, we can have some breakfast and I can explain what I was doin', even though I'm not obligated. A ranger doesn't have to explain his comin' and goins."

They were the first customers and had barely sat down when the heavyset woman who owned the place was right there with fresh, hot coffee. "What'll it be, folks? I have... Oh my God, you're the fella that whipped that no good Jack Baldwin! This whole town owes you a debt of thanks. For several weeks now the whole town was afraid to walk down the same side of the street he was on, he was that mean."

Clay waved his arm and said, "Please, no gratitude is needed. I..."

"Well you sure earned it," the woman said, "And breakfast is on me!"

"Oh, no it ain't," Loralie said, standing up. "It was my honor he was pertectin' and I'm the one thet is buyin' breakfast!"

Without a word, Clay stood up and headed for the door.

"Where you goin'?" Loralie asked, speaking to his back.

Clay stopped, took a deep breath, then turned around. He was in no condition to yell because it would cause him more pain than he was already in, so he spoke quietly through his swollen lips.

"I came in here to have some breakfast, not watch two hens get their feathers ruffled. I can and will pay for my meals, either here, or somewhere else. Now, which will it be?"

Loralie's lips formed into a pout and she stomped her foot, then sat down. "You are the most stubborn man I've ever knowed."

The owner of the restaurant, picked up his coffee and said, "I'll get you a fresh cup of coffee, Mister Ranger Man."

Clay knew he wasn't yet up to heavy chewing, so he ordered biscuits and gravy, and when it came, it was on a large platter with enough for two hungry cowboys.

Clay looked at the huge platter of food and decided he may have won the battle, but she had won the war.

During breakfast, Clay related everything that had gone on since they'd last seen each other, and then Loralie did the same, leaving nothing out.

"Wow," Clay said. "After all that, I'm surprised you needed help with that Baldwin, fella."

"Oh…? He was not only big, but he was powerful strong, too. If'n you hadn't ah come along, he might'a had his way with me, but it wouldn't ah been easy and I had plans of my own about what I was gonna do to him if'n he got me to his camp."

Clay had no doubt Loralie Benson would be a woman to be reckoned with, whether it be coming to a man or pushing him away. At some point, Jack would have left himself vulnerable and she would have been waiting to take advantage of the situation. Pictures reeled in his mind, but he kept them to himself. Instead, he changed the subject.

"So, you're headed home to start rebuildin'?"

"Yup," she said, "An this time it ain't gonna be no log cabin, no sir'ee. I'm gonna build me ah big house thet I can be proud of. I'll have me some fine horses, maybe hi-breds. The name, Loralie Benson is gonna mean somethin'."

"And what about the Mullins?" Clay asked.

"I'll hire me some of those Hacker boys. They's good with horses, cattle, and fightin'."

Clay sat and looked at this young woman who, instead of cryin' an goin' to pieces because of her parent's death, she'd picked herself up and faced the challenge ahead of her with determination. She knew horses and cattle, and if things were different... he thought to himself, then let the idea slip away into the recess of his mind. He had a bank robber and murderer to find and arrest.

Clay looked out of the window. The sun was coming up over the tops of the buildings, proving to be another scorcher. He scooted his chair back and stood up. "I'm burnin' daylight, and I've got an outlaw to apprehend, so I guess we should say our goodbyes here," not wanting to mention the fact that they would probably be on the same train.

Loralie stood up and stared him straight in the eyes. "You've got ah woman ta contend with, right here, first. I still got two hours afore the train leaves and I plan on spendin' them seein' ta your wounds, and I don't want no argument. You ain't in no shape fer outlaw chasin', yet. You can catch ah train tomorrow, if'n yer up to it."

Clay had to admit the cloths soaked in Epson salt water she was putting on his face, hands and side made the pain much easier to deal with. After an hour and a half of her tendin' his wounds, the swelling was beginning to go down and the discoloration on his skin had faded a little.

It took a bit of doin', but Clay finally convinced Loralie to catch her train and not wait until he was better, which he had to admit, would take at least another day.

Their parting was awkward to say the least. Standing on the platform near her train car, Clay looked into her eyes and felt his knees go weak. She had lips that invited a man to kiss them, and he was about to fall to temptation, when Loralie took charge of the situation by reaching up and kissing him on the lips, then turned and ran for the train.

The kiss was sweet and tender and lasted just long enough to set Clay on fire.

The last he saw of her was her face in the window of the train as it pulled away.

When he turned around, Walt and Cynthia were standing there. Walt was shaking his head from side to side and grinning like a mischievous boy who'd just gotten away with something.

"You do lead an exciting life, my friend, yes sir, an exciting life."

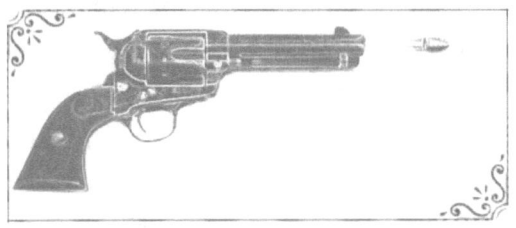

CHAPTER SEVEN

By the time the train pulled into Memphis, Loralie Benson was tired of traveling and was eager to get back to her Cinch Mountain and the cool breeze coming through the trees and the sound of night owls lulling her to sleep.

By her calculation, Knoxville was still close to four hundred miles away, with Nashville sittin' somewhere in the middle. "If'in there ain't no more delays, I still got four more days of train ridin't ta do," she said with a sigh, "then a full day on horseback afore I can get back home, safe and sound."

The train would only be in Memphis for thirty minutes or so, so there was no need to get off, she thought as she watched some of the passengers leaving the train.

Suddenly, all of her senses came alive and her stomach began to do flip-flops. Standing on the platform was a real looker of a woman. She was elaborately dressed and was wearing a wide brimmed hat with feathers sticking out of it. The dress she was wearing fit like she'd been poured into it and her face was painted up like one of the harlots she'd read about in them dime novels.

Loralie had no doubt, this was the female outlaw Clay was looking for and for reasons she didn't try to think about, she grabbed her bag and left the train.

Loralie stepped onto the platform and stopped, looking around as though she was looking for someone and her eyes met those of Lottie Simmons for just a moment, then moved on.

Lottie saw the striking young woman and moved toward her. As she approached the young lady, she asked, "Excuse me, are you Lillie Tomlin?"

Loralie turned and looked Lottie squarely in the eyes and felt a shiver run up her spine. The woman may be all gussied up, but her eyes told a different tale. They were cold, hard eyes that said this was a woman to be feared.

"Sorry, but you have the wrong person. My name is Loralie Benson and I'm just passin' through," Loralie said with a broad smile.

"Too bad," Lottie said, obviously disappointed.

Loralie's mind was running a hundred miles a minute. Her instinct told her this was the woman Clay was looking for, but she wasn't sure what to do about it.

"I'm sorry. I was waiting for someone and I hoped you were her," Lottie said, touching her arm lightly. "You say you're just passing through? Too bad I could use a girl pretty as you."

Loralie turned and stared at Lottie again, an idea forming in her mind. "Really? What kind of work would that be?" Loralie asked innocently.

Lottie stared at her for a moment then said, "My name is Lottie Simmons. I own a saloon here in town and I have girls working for me who entertain the men who come there looking for excitement."

"Oh, you mean..." Loralie exclaimed as if she were shocked. "I've never done anything like that. I mean, I wouldn't even know where to begin... I've, I've..."

Lottie got an astonished look on her face. "You mean to tell me? How old are you, darlin'?"

"If'n you must know, I'm twenty-three and back in the hills of Tennessee where I growed up there weren't many men-folk callers. Papa would run'um off afore they could even step down from their horse."

Lottie smiled. "Well maybe we could start you off downstairs. Can you sing or dance?"

"Ma said I have a fair ta meddlin' voice, but the only songs I know is mountain songs, like, Rye Whiskey and Way Up On Cinch Mountain, you know, songs like that. Oh, and I can do the Cinch Mountain back step. That's dancin'," Loralie said.

Lottie looked at the beautiful young lady standing in front of her and wondered if she was for real, or just pulling her leg. After a moment, she decided the girl was on the level and made a decision. The men would climb all over each other to get close to her. She had a beautiful face, a nice body and that flaming red hair… With her hair combed out and in a green dress, it wouldn't matter what she sang or whether she could even sing or not, they would clamor all over themselves just to look at her. She would be money in the bank.

"If you don't mind my asking, why are you just passing through? Do you have someone waiting for you?"

"No ma'am, I got neither of them things. I'm jest goin' home," Loralie said, not wanting to give away the reason she got off the train in the first place. And why had she? Clay would be here in a day or so and he could arrest her then. But what if she took off again sos she could rob another bank. No, she decided. It would be best if she stayed here and kept an eye on Miss Lottie Simmons.

"Well, if you can delay your trip, I would like you to come and sing at my place. I will pay you ten dollars a night to just sing a few songs and entertain the men in general, you know, talk to them so they will buy more drinks. You won't have to go upstairs if you don't want to," Lottie said with a smile.

When Loralie looked skeptical, Lottie added, "And that will include room and board."

What better way to keep an eye on her than to be right there in her saloon, Loralie thought, and get paid for doing it.

"I surely could use some extra money," Loralie said in her best grateful voice. "I guess it wouldn't hurt ta stay around for a while, if'n all I got ta do is sing and jabber jaw with the men-folk."

"It's settled then," Lottie said with the radiant smile of someone who had just won big at the poker table.

· Lottie took Loralie by the arm and headed toward town, feeling like a gold mine had just been dropped in her lap.

"Let's get you settled and then I can show you around," Lottie said, feeling very proud of herself.

Loralie was feeling proud of herself, as well. She hoped Clay would appreciate what she was doing for him.

The green dress fit Loralie like it had been made for her and she told Lottie this was the prettiest dress she'd ever had, which wasn't a lie, since it was only the second dress she'd ever had on, but she left that part out.

Lottie smiled. Before she was done with this little girl, she would turn her into the highest priced call girl in Memphis.

In Loralie's room, Lottie said, "You don't start work until eight this evening, which gives you the rest of the day to rest or just wander around town. There's a bathtub and hot water just two doors down from here, to your right."

Dressed again in her flowered dress, Loralie strolled down the sidewalk, taking in the town, all the while, looking for the sheriff's office. Maybe he could arrest Lottie and hold her for Clay until he got to town, which she hoped would be tomorrow.

She saw the sign indicating the sheriff's office on the opposite side of the street. A few doors beyond, was a mercantile store.

Without seeming to be in a hurry, Loralie crossed the street and sauntered down the sidewalk, glancing around to see how many people were out. She smiled - Memphis was a busy town.

Before entering the sheriff's office, Loralie casually walked past and glanced in the front window. The sheriff was sitting at his desk reading. He looked up and smiled, then nodded his head. Loralie smiled back and kept walking.

The mercantile store smelled of spice, tobacco and new leather. The place was filled from floor to ceiling with everthing a person could ever want. They sure could use a store like this in Cinch Mountain. They had a mercantile store but not like this one.

She decided to treat herself and picked up some toilet articles for her bath. The lady behind the counter told her she had used the same brand and would recommend them highly. Loralie figured if she was going to look like a lady, she might as well smell like one too.

Loralie turned and walked out just behind three women, who turned in the direction of the sheriff's office. The street was crowded with people and no one noticed as Loralie opened the door of the sheriff's office and quickly stepped inside.

The sheriff looked up and smiled. Even sitting down, she could tell he was a large man. Typical of the times, he sported a large, bushy moustache and a full head of unruly, black hair. An ugly looking scar ran down across the left side of his cheek. But it was his eyes that she noticed most. They were deep blue with little flakes of silver and he had an honest face.

The sheriff stood up and said, "Good mornin', Sunshine. I'm Sheriff Buck Tyler, what troubles could a pretty young lady like you have, other than ever man in town chasin' after you?"

Trying not to blush, Loralie went right to the reason she was here. "Got ah question," she said. "If there was someone here in town that was wanted by the Texas Rangers, and a ranger was comin' ta town soon, could you put that person in yer jail and hold'm till the ranger got here in, say, a day or so?"

"Now that's ah right curious question," he said as he walked over and refilled his coffee cup. "Coffee?" he asked.

"Thank you, no," Loralie said, then waited for him to answer her question.

The sheriff pointed to the wall behind his desk and asked, "Do you see that person's picture on the wall, there?"

Loralie walked over and looked at the dozen or so pictures pinned to the wall, but did not see a picture of Lottie.

She turned back and said, "No sir, I surely don't. Does that make a difference?"

"Makes all the difference in the world," he said, then blew on his coffee before taking a sip. "It's a matter of jurisdiction. If I don't have paper on someone, they're free to come and go as long as they don't break any laws here in town. Now if this ranger was to bring somebody in and ask me to hold that person for him for a few days, I could do that, but otherwise, my hands are tied."

Loralie's disappointment must have showed on her face because the sheriff asked, "Has this outlaw you speak of bothered you in any way that I might need to arrest him for?"

This time Loralie's face did redden and she said, "No, and thank you for your time."

The sheriff watched her go and wondered how a pretty, young lady like that could be mixed up with Texas Rangers and outlaws?

He walked back to his desk and sat down. Setting his coffee aside, he picked up the piece of paper he'd been reading before the young lady came in. At the top of the page there was a name, LOTTIE SIMMONS, and below was list of laws he hoped one day she would break so he could shut her down. The city council had been on his back to close her down, but so far, Lottie walked that thin line between working just within the law and stepping over the boundary. She was smart. He knew she kept a copy of city and state laws in her office.

Until certain laws against drinking, gambling and prostitution were enacted, his hands were tied. And he had to admit she ran a tight house. Her dealers were smart and never got caught. The tables, though in the houses favor, were not rigged that he knew of. She had six bad hombres to see that there was no fights or gunplay going on; and she kept a doctor on her payroll to make sure her girls were clean and inspected once a week. He knew she was cheating the customers, but so far he hadn't been able to catch her, yet.

Once out of the sheriff's office, Loralie went straight back to Lottie's Place and took a nice, hot bath, then climbed between the sheets and slept until six o'clock that evening.

At seven that evening, dressed in her new green dress, and her hair brushed out like Lottie had suggested, Loralie went down to have some supper before beginning her first night's work.

Lottie was there and looked pleased when Loralie walked in. She waved Loralie over and introduced her to the half dozen working girls.

Loralie looked them over and was surprised. She didn't know much about women of the night, but she'd heard stories and these women were nothing like the women in the tales the men back home told. These women were clean and well dressed and acted like ladies. There was more to this Lottie Simmons than met the eye.

The women ranged from around eighteen, up to thirty-five. They were very pleasant and told her if she needed anything just ask.

At eight o'clock that evening, Loralie stood in the doorway of an anteroom waiting for Lottie to introduce her. Her hands were beginning to sweat and she felt like she might throw up. She was about to bolt, when she heard Lottie calling for her to come up to the piano.

As she walked across the floor, something came over her and she smiled and waved at the men who were hooting and whistling, her hips taking on a mind of their own.

The piano player was a small-framed man with a pencil thin mustache. He was dressed in a tan gabardine suit, and sported an Irish derby. "Do you know, Cinch Mountain Mama?" she asked as she leaned an elbow on the top of the piano.

"Sure," he said as he sat his cigarette in an ashtray and started the intro.

Why she chose this particular song to open with she wasn't sure, but the men whooped and hollered and each one of them walked over and dropped money in an empty cigar box sitting on top of the piano.

All but one smiled and winked as they walked past her. The one man who didn't, stopped for a moment and stared at her before he went back to his seat. Loralie thought for just a moment there was recognition in his eyes, but that couldn't be, she'd never been in Memphis before. When she looked down, she saw he had dropped a ten-dollar bill in the box. Now that was really strange. She hoped it wasn't in reference to him having something else in mind, later on.

The night finally ended for her about two in the morning and Loralie was dead tired. She had talked to almost every man in the place, except the strange man who sat alone in the corner of the room.

Just as the last of the customers were leaving, the strange man approached her and lifted his hat and asked, "Are you Loralie Benson from Cinch Mountain?"

Well, you could have knocked Loralie over with a feather, she was that shocked, and after a long pause, she said, "Am I supposed ta know you?"

The man smiled and said, "No. But I know you from when I used to deal with your pa back in Knoxville, when he'd come down off the mountain. He talked about you a lot and described you to a tee. Plus, you look a lot like him, only prettier," he said with a small chuckle.

When she just continued to stare at him, he said, "My name is Price Woodard and your pa and I used to do business together. I'm a horse buyer. Your pa raised some fine horses. Sorry to hear what happened. Is that why you're working here? Heard the Mullins took over the place after you left."

If Loralie had been shocked before, she was even more shocked over this bit of news. Her knees got weak and suddenly it was hard to breathe. "What do you mean, the Mullins took over my land? I ain't sold that land ta nobody and don't intend to."

Price Woodard shook his head and said, "I don't know the details, only what I heard and read."

He reached into the inside pocket of his coat and pulled out a folded-up poster and handed it to her.

Loralie unfolded the poster and almost fainted. In bold letters, it said,

-MULLIN'S CINCH MOUNTAIN
LUMBER COMPANY –
GRAND OPENING SOON
THE BEST LUMBER ON THE MOUNTAIN AT
REASONABLE PRICES

It took Loralie a minute or so to absorb the information she'd just read. She handed the poster back to the man and asked, "When did you get this?"

"Just this morning. A man was walking around town tacking them up wherever he could. I asked him where all he had put up the posters, and he said every town between here and Knoxville. Because of what I'd heard about your folks being killed by Indians, I asked him if that was the old Benson place, and he said it was. According to him, the land had been abandoned and the Mullins family moved onto the land and had taken possession. He said his name was Jeff Mullins. Do you know him?"

"Yes, I know him." Loralie felt the heat climbing up her spine. Anger was building inside her like a hurricane headed for land. "Those people are tryin' ta steal my land! I didn't abandon it. And I didn't sell it. I jest went off for ah spell ta raise some money so's I can rebuild the place. I even tole the sheriff I'd only be gone ah few months."

Price Woodard shook his head, again and asked, "What can I do to help? Do you need money?"

Loralie took a good look at Price Woodard. He was taller than her, maybe a shade over six feet. He had a nice face and was dressed in a dark suit, and maybe only a few years younger than her pa had been.

"Thank ya, but there ain't nothin' nobody can do but me. I need ta get back there and throw them Mullins off'n my property afore they start cuttin' down my trees. I promised pa I would take care of the place an I aim ta do jest that."

After thanking Price Woodard again, Loralie went to her room and packed her things, leaving out the worn-out buckskins and boots. Being a lady would have to wait. She was about to go to war.

All packed and dressed in her buckskins, she laid down on the bed to get some rest. There wasn't anything she could do until daylight except try and figure out a reason to get Lottie arrested so she would be here when Clay arrived.

Bright and early the next morning, Loralie was down at the train station buying her ticket for Knoxville. She left her bag with the station man, then went to have breakfast at the small diner just down the street. It was already getting crowded when she walked in.

The first person she saw was, Sheriff Buck Tyler. He was sitting alone, just finishing his breakfast.

Loralie walked over to his table and sat down without being asked. She was on a mission and meant to have done with it.

At first, the sheriff didn't recognize her dressed in buckskins with a handgun hanging on her hip. He watched as she leaned her rifle against the table.

"Don't suppose you recognize me not bein' all gussied up. I'm Loralie Benson. I was by your office yesterday."

The sheriff smiled and shook his head. "Even in buckskins you look mighty pretty. Mind telling me why you're dressed this way and packing that pistol and rifle?"

Loralie ignored his question and asked a question of her own. "When does the sheriff's, office open up?"

The sheriff took a sip of his coffee and then looked over at the pretty redhead dressed in buckskins. "Soon as I finish my coffee," he said wondering what the woman was up to?

"Thank you," she said, then stood up, picked up her rifle and walked over and took a chair at the counter.

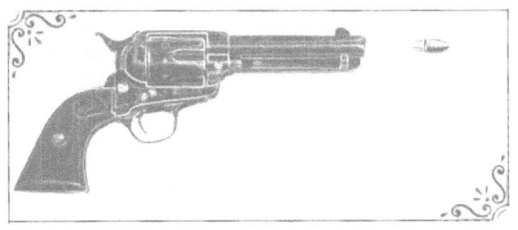

CHAPTER EIGHT

Clay Brentwood was standing on the landing between the passenger cars, enjoying the swaying motion of the train and the cool morning breeze against his face. He had been up for two hours, had breakfast, several cups of coffee and now was having a smoke, while trying to set up a plan in his mind. The local law would be the first place to stop. A woman like Lottie Simmons was not the kind of woman to go unnoticed. After all, she was trying to build a reputation to equal Belle Starr, the most famous female outlaw the west had to offer at the present time, and from what he'd heard, Lottie was working hard to top her.

What if he was wrong and she wasn't in Memphis? What if it was just another stopover? Somehow his mind couldn't accept that. The woman had to have a base of operation somewhere and Memphis seemed an ideal place. According to what he'd heard, it was a wide-open town and if she kept her nose clean, she would be free to run all over the west and raise all sorts of hell, then hightail it back to where there was no paper on her.

She might even own a legitimate business and be a respected citizen; however, he doubted that last part.

If she did take the money from the robberies and invest it, it would have to be something that pulled in a high return, like, liquor, women or gambling, which amounted to owning a saloon or house of ill repute, which meant putting her in the limelight, yet skirting the edge of the law. Now, that sounded more like the woman he was seeking.

Clay ground the stub of his cigarette between his thumb and first finger, then tossed the ashes to the wind. After taking one more breath of fresh air, he walked back into the car and stopped dead in his tracks.

Down near the middle of the aisle, two men were throwing punches at each other. Or better still, one was throwing punches and the other one was holding up his arms to try and ward off the other man's assaulting blows.

The one throwing the punches was a big man, dressed in a black suit and seemed to be beating on a man about half his size.

The other man was slight of build and definitely not a brawler. He looked to be less than twenty years old and was dressed like a cowhand. A wide brimmed hat was laying a few feet behind him on the floor, and unlike most men of the day, he wasn't wearing a side arm.

The big man had the smaller man by the hair and drove his fist into the young man's face, which sent him onto the floor, flat of his back, blood running from his mouth.

Sitting in a seat near the fight sat a young woman with raven black hair and dark eyes. By the way she was dressed, she looked to be of Spanish origin. Her eyes were wide with fright and she was clutching a small bag in her hands.

Suddenly, her eyes got even bigger and she yelled, "Por favor! Do not kill him!"

Clay's attention had been on the young woman and therefore had not seen the big man pull a pistol.

The big man pointed the pistol at the young man lying on the floor and said in a gravelly voice, "Now you're gonna die, cowboy."

The young man stared up at him in horror. He was going to die without being able to defend himself. Why had he listened to his ma when she told him if he didn't wear a gun, no one would have reason to shoot at him.

Instinct took Clay the few steps to reach the big man and shove his arm upward just as he pulled the trigger, putting a hole in the ceiling.

"What the?" the big man said, whirling to face Clay.

Again, instinct took over and his hand went to his own pistol and when the man turned, he was looking down the barrel of Clay's big forty-four.

"I don't want to kill you, mister, but if you raise that pistol in my direction, it'll be the last thing you ever do. Now toss it onto the seat to your left."

The big man's eyes were blazing daggers and there was no doubt he wanted to kill Clay but was wise enough to see that he was standing at deaths door if he tried.

After a moment, the big man tossed his thirty-eight-caliber pistol onto the seat, then said, "You got no right buttin' in, mister. This no good cowboy deserves ta die for what he did."

"And just what did he do?" Clay asked.

"He made advances toward my fiancé," the big man said, nodding his head toward the young man, who by now was standing up.

Clay looked at the young man and asked, "Is that true?"

The young man turned and picked up his hat, brushed his hair back with his fingers, then jammed his hat back onto his head.

He wiped blood from his nose and mouth with a red handkerchief, then looked Clay in the eyes. "No sir, It is not."

"Well just for the record, what did you do to get this man so riled up?"

The young man looked at the woman, then back at Clay. "I was walkin' down the aisle on my way to the dinin' car and happened ta notice this pretty lady sittin' in her seat. She looked up as I went by and I lifted my hat and said, good mornin', just bein' respectful like my ma taught me. The next thing I knew, this pea brained brawler jumped up and began accusin' me of makin' advances toward his woman.

"I tried to explain that I was just bein' polite, but he wouldn't hear of it and began clubbin' me with them ham hock fists of his. The next thing I knew, I was on the floor and lookin' down the barrel of his pistol. Then you came along."

Clay turned his head and looked at the young woman. "Is that what happened?"

Her eyes went to the big man and Clay saw fear in them that slowly changed to defiance. Squaring her shoulders, she looked at Clay and said, "It is as he said, Senor, he did nothing disrespectful. He only tipped his hat and said good morning."

Clay looked back at the big man and asked, "And this is why you wanted to kill a man?"

"It wasn't what he done, it was what he was thinkin'. It might'a been good mornin' that came out of his mouth, but it was something else he had on his mind."

Clay couldn't believe what he was hearing. The young man was right, this brawler had to have a brain no bigger than a pea. The young lady was very pretty, but to be so jealous that a smile or good morning would cause you to kill someone, was more than he could fathom.

"And you say this young lady is your fiancé?"

"She shore is. Won her fair and square in ah poker game with her pa," the man said with pride.

"And just how much did her father owe you?" Clay asked.

"Sixty-four dollars," the big man said.

Clay turned to the young lady and asked, "Do you want to marry this man?"

The young woman's jaw tightened and her eyes blazed fire as she stared at him. "No Senor, the man is a brute and he cheated my father at the poker table. My father is no gambler and was afraid of this man, so he gave me, his only child, to this man over a poker debt. I could not believe he did such a thing and from that day on, I no longer have a father."

"And just how did he cheat your father?" Clay asked.

"I was sitting off to the side and this man would look away from the table at some imaginary thing. My father would look to see what it was and when he did, this man would deal cards to himself from the bottom of the deck. I saw him do it several times. I knew he was cheating but there was nothing I could do."

"She's lyin'. I ain't never cheated at cards, never had to, I'm just naturally lucky."

Clay almost laughed out loud at this statement, but held himself in check. This was serious business; a woman's life was at stake.

Clay thought for just a moment, then reached into his pocket and pulled out a wad of bills and counted off sixty-four dollars and stuffed the money in the breast pocket of the man's suit coat. "That should take care of your loss, and now the young lady belongs to me," Clay said with a grin.

"What about her train fare? That cost me three dollars."

"Let's just say you gambled and lost," Clay whispered, as he stared the man down.

The man looked down at the woman, then back at the hole at the end of Clay's pistol.

"She ain't worth getting shot over," he said and stormed off down the aisle and left the car, leaving his pistol on the seat.

The young woman was staring at Clay with hard eyes. "So, I am passed from one man to another. How does that make things any better?"

"Sorry you got the wrong impression," Clay said. "You're free to go wherever you want. I just wanted to help get you out of a bad situation."

"What about the money you paid for me?" the young woman asked, defiance once again in her voice.

Clay took a pencil and piece of paper from the inside pocket of his coat and wrote his name and the address of his bank on it, then handed it to her.

"If you ever get into a position where you have extra money, you can repay me. Send it to the address on that piece of paper," he said, nodding his head toward the paper she held in her hand.

"Do you have someplace to go to?" Clay asked.

"No Senor," she said. "I will get off in Memphis and find a job. I do not want to go back to where my father is, not after what he did to me."

During the awkward silence that followed, the young man spoke up. "Beggin' yore pardin', but if you're lookin' for work, I got a small place not far from Memphis and I am in dire need of somebody ta help with the cookin' and house cleanin'. Can you cook and clean house?"

The young woman looked up at him and smiled. "Si, I am a very good cook and I can clean house."

The young man pulled off his hat and said, "Well, it's like this; I ain't much of ah cook and after ah long day of tendin' ta my place, well, I don't have much energy fer cleanin' or cookin'. I can't pay much more'n room and board til some money starts comin' in, but you'd have yer own room and I'll be right respectful of you."

The young woman looked up at Clay, who smiled and nodded his head.

When he left the car, they were sitting side by side.

"Name's Ryan Tate and I got me ah grandson from the great horse, Alan Black, bought him for a pittance of what he's worth, from a man who was down on his luck. I Inherited five hundred acres of land from an aunt I never knew, and I've been workin' and savin' my money for three years now. I'm on my way back from Texas where I got me six Spanish Mustang mares. And in a few years, I'm gonna own the finest Tennessee Walking Horses in the state," he said, proudly.

"My name is Consquella Anna Maria Lopez and you will come home to a clean house every night and have a good meal waiting for you."

CHAPTER NINE

At a few minutes to eleven that morning, Clay stepped off the train in Memphis and looked around, not realizing Loralie had been there and gone, already.

Ryan and Consquella came off the train and walked, arm in arm, toward the train car where the animals were loaded, the same place he would be going to get his horse. She was looking up at the young Ryan and laughing at something he'd just said.

Clay sighed, remembering how happy he and his wife had been before the outlaw Curly Beeler and his gang had raided their ranch and raped and killed her and their unborn child.

The sound of the ramp being lowered brought Clay back to the present and he headed in that direction.

As Clay led the big stallion down the ramp, he saw Ryan leading six mares tied together in a string. The young man waited until Clay got close and handed the lead rope to Consquella.

"You left afore I got ah chance ta thank ya for what you did," the young man said, sticking out his hand. "Ryan Tate."

"No thanks needed. Hope things work out," Clay said, accepting the handshake. "Those are some fine lookin' mustang mares you got there. You plannin' on doin' some breedin'?"

Young Ryan Tate explained the whole story to Clay, then added, "You ever need anything, anything at all, you just give ah holler and I'll come ah runnin', you here?"

Clay stepped onto the saddle, put two fingers to his hat in the direction of Consquella and said, "Ma'am, I truly hope everything works out for you," and to Ryan, he said "You take good care of her so I don't have to come callin', you hear?"

As Clay rode down the street he was amazed. This had started out as an Indian village and now, because of the cotton industry, it was turning into a major trading center. He'd read somewhere that just a few years back, in '78' and '79' there had been an outburst of yellow fever that had killed nearly five thousand people and the city had gone bankrupt. But because of the cotton and lumber boom, the city bounced back and was growing by leaps and bounds.

On the left, Clay saw the sheriff's sign swinging in the breeze, but what really got his attention was a sign a ways on further and on the right side of the street announcing,

LOTTIE'S PLACE
WHISKEY, GAMBLING AND GIRLS

Just then, Clay heard some loud yelling comin' from the direction of the sheriff's office, and when he turned his attention back, he saw six men with pistols drawn, standing in front. The biggest of the six men was standing slightly in front of the others and seemed to be the one in charge

"Turn her loose and we promise not to kill you, Sheriff. Otherwise, you die and she goes free anyway."

Clay watched as a rifle barrel came through a small slot in the door, followed by a gruff voice. "If I go down, some of you will go with me, and you'll be the first, Bull."

That stopped them while they held a pow-wow. The big man said something and pointed, then one of the men turned and started toward the mercantile store.

Clay wasn't sure what was going on but it involved a lawman and that made it his business too. Seemed like one man against six - not the best of odds for the sheriff.

He rode the black stallion over to the mercantile store, stepped down and followed the man into the store, just a few steps behind him.

The man didn't seem to be much without his gun. He pointed it at the man behind the counter and said, "Dynamite. Get me some dynamite and be quick about it old man."

Clay slammed his rifle barrel down across his arm, causing the pistol to fall from his hand, and before the man could respond, Clay raised the rifle and brought the barrel down across his skull.

The man slumped to the floor without a sound. Clay looked at the man behind the counter and said, "Tie him up and put a gag in his mouth. I'll be back ta get'em shortly."

The storeowner was standing wide eyed when Clay went out the back door and climbed the stairs to the roof of the building taking two at a time.

From the front of the building Clay had a good view of the street and the men standing in front of the sheriff's office. He raised his rifle to his shoulder, took aim and shot the man in front in the knee, then yelled. "Hold it right there!"

At the sight of the big man on the ground, groaning and holding his leg, they froze.

"Sheriff!" Clay called out. "If they don't drop their guns by the count of three, you take the ones in the front and I'll take the ones in the rear. One…"

That was as far as he got before they were tossing their pistols into the dirt.

Clay wasted no time getting down the back stairs and through the mercantile store where he picked up the unconscious man and tossed him over his shoulder.

Out on the street, Clay dropped the unconscious man, unceremoniously on the ground.

The door opened and the sheriff walked out with a rifle in his hands. He stopped on the sidewalk, grinned and said, "You must be Brentwood."

Clay looked at the sheriff and said, "I am, but how do you know that?"

"You happen to know a young, redheaded spitfire by the name of Loralie Benson?"

Clay nodded and wondered what she was up to now, but first things first. He helped the sheriff herd the men into a row of cells at the back of the office. Off to one end, in a cell all by herself, a woman dressed in her nightclothes called out through the bars. "You'll never get away with this, Buck. I got friends! Friends in high places!"

Clay noticed the woman was sporting ah black eye and wondered if she might be Lottie Simmons? Looked like there might be a story here and he was anxious to hear it.

Back in the sheriff's office, Buck poured them both a cup of coffee and handed one to Clay.

"Name's Buck Tyler, I'm the law here in Memphis. That Loralie Benson is some gal, some gal indeed."

"I can't argue with you there, but how do you know her and why did she mention my name?" Clay asked, sipping the strong, black coffee.

Buck walked around his desk and sat down in his chair and shook his head, a big grin appearing on his face, causing the scar on his cheek to wrinkle more than it already was.

"She came in here yesterday morning, looking pretty as a picture, asking me if I could put someone, she didn't say who, in my jail until you got here today. I had her look at the wanted posters to see if the person she was talking about might be up there, but she said, no."

Buck reached into his shirt pocket and pulled out a sack of Bull Durham tobacco and some papers and commenced to build himself a smoke while he talked. "I told her if the person wasn't wanted in my town, I couldn't just arrest them on somebody's word unless that person had done something to them or they had a warrant. She said, she didn't. So, I told her there wasn't anything I could do and she left."

"So, that was it?" Clay asked.

Buck grinned even bigger and said, "Not by a long shot. This morning, while I was having my breakfast, she comes into the café, dressed in buckskins, carrying a rifle and had a pistol strapped on her side. I almost didn't recognize her. She walked up to my table and asked when my office would be open. I said, as soon as I finished my coffee. Then she went over and sat at the counter and ordered breakfast for herself. After I finished my coffee I came over and opened up, wondering what she was up to."

A glimmer of an idea was beginning to form in Clay's mind, especially after seeing that woman locked up in the cell, who had to be Lottie, but he wanted to hear the rest of the story, it sounded like it was gonna be ah good one. "So what happened then?"

"Now this is where it really gets interesting," Buck said as he lit his cigarette and blew a stream of smoke into the air. "After she left my office yesterday morning, she somehow got herself a job, singing over at Lottie's place."

Clay almost choked on his coffee and said, "What? I didn't know she could sing."

"Well, apparently, she can, and from what I understand, she's pretty good at it too. Anyway, according to Loralie, the only reason she took the job was to keep an eye on Lottie Simmons until you got here."

Clay sat his cup on the sheriff's desk. "Is Loralie still here?"

"Hang on, partner, this is where it really gets interesting."

Clay looked at the sheriff and wondered what else could have happened.

The sheriff took a sip of coffee, then said, "Apparently, she got some disturbing news about her piece of land up north of Knoxville and decided to catch the early train this morning."

"Then why did she want to know when your office opened?" Clay asked, thinking he already knew the answer.

"I'm coming to that," the sheriff said. "From the way I understand it, she was worried that Lottie, the woman you're looking for, might get away before you got here, so she went into her bedroom and dragged her out of bed and hauled her in here, claiming Lottie had tried to kill her and wanted to sign a complaint against her."

"Tried to kill her? Why?" Clay asked trying to understand Loralie's train of thought. "And is that how Lottie got the black eye?"

The sheriff chuckled and said, "This part is really interesting. According to Loralie, Lottie came into her room and tried to force herself on her and Loralie told her, no. And that's when Lottie supposedly attacked Loralie and tried to kill her. During the scuffle, Loralie apparently punched her in the eye."

Clay stood up and paced the room, his brain envisioning the fight. It was all he could do not to laugh out loud.

"Course, Lottie told a different story," the sheriff said. "But since Loralie was filing a complaint, I had no choice but to lock Lottie up. I told Lottie they could battle out their stories in court."

"Do you believe Loralie's story?" Clay asked.

The sheriff put out what was left of his cigarette in a jar lid turned upside down, that he used for an ashtray. "Don't really matter, does it? She got Lottie locked up until you got here like she wanted in the first place, and I figure your warrant will be enough for me to turn her over to you, which takes care of Loralie's case until Lottie comes back, if she ever does. Besides, I've been trying for some time to find a way to shut Lottie down, but she's slick, and stays one step ahead of the law, if you know what I mean. I know the mayor will be happy to see her gone."

Clay finished his coffee and sat the empty cup on the sheriff's desk, then reached inside his shirt pocket and pulled out a piece of paper.

"The warrant ain't exactly like what you're used to, but it's legal. The sheriff back in Fort Smith, Arkansas hand wrote it while we were out on the trail, chasin' Lottie and her gang for robbin' the bank. She killed one of her own gang cause his horse threw ah shoe and was slowin' her down. We caught her gang but she got away. They confessed the whole thing. He wrote out that warrant and I've been doggin' her trail ever since."

Buck studied the hand-written warrant and let out a sigh. It was true, he'd never seen one like this before, but hell, the man was a Texas Ranger, not some John Doe citizen who might be nursin' ah grudge. And even though he was a few miles outside his jurisdiction, the man had no reason to lie.

"I'll accept this," Buck said, handing the hand-written warrant back to Clay.

"What about those men who were tryin' ta break her outta jail?" Clay asked.

"Oh, I imagine they'll get six months on the prison farm for threatening an officer of the law," Buck said. "Should give you enough time to get Lottie settled into an Arkansas prison."

"What's gonna happen to her saloon, now that she'll no longer be around?"

Buck grinned and walked over to the stove and refilled his cup, then lifted the pot in Clay's direction. Clay shook his head, no, and waited until the sheriff got back to his desk and sat down.

"Both the mayor and I know," Buck began, "that she's got crooked dealers, her girls steal money from the men while they're asleep and the whiskey is watered down, but she's slick enough to not get caught doing it. So, if she leaves the state for say, six months, then the city can take possession of it and I can buy it."

"You want to buy it?" Clay said, somewhat amused.

"I promised the mayor and the city council I would clean the place up. I've got some money put by and we have already settled on a price, along with a percentage going to the city ever month. I guess you might say the city will be my silent partner, cept'n we don't want the ladies church group knowing about it. They might not see it the same way me and the mayor do."

"I see," Clay said as he stood up. "I'd like ta see Lottie if you don't mind. Need ta make this all official like."

The sheriff stood up and walked with Clay back to her cell.

Lottie got off her bunk and walked up to the bars and said, "Well, did you come to turn me loose?"

The sheriff rubbed the stubble of beard on his cheek and said. "No. I brought someone in who wants to talk to you."

"Are you Lottie Simmons?" Clay asked before introductions were made.

"That's right, and who are you?" Lottie asked, placing a hand on her hip.

"Name's Clay Brentwood, I'm ah Texas Ranger and I have ah warrant for your arrest; murder and bank robbery back in Fort Smith, Arkansas," Clay said, touching the warrant in his shirt pocket.

Lottie looked at him and grinned. "You're a long way from Texas, Mister Ranger man, and way outta your jurisdiction, so that piece of paper don't mean ah hill of beans here in Tennessee. Arkansas, you say? Never been there."

She then turned her attention to the sheriff and said, "Now, if you're through wastin' my time, you can open that door so I can get outta here."

Technically she was right, the ranger was out of his jurisdiction and the warrant was from Arkansas. He turned and looked at Clay for help.

Clay nodded his head at the sheriff and turned his attention back to Lottie. "In that case, you can think of me as a bounty hunter, which allows me to go anywhere in pursuit of criminals I have paper on. And since I have paper on you, I arrest you for murdering Joseph Allen and robbin' the bank in Fort Smith, Arkansas."

Lottie turned and looked at the sheriff, disbelief on her face. "You gonna let him get away with this?" she asked.

"The man has a warrant and bounty hunters have no jurisdiction limits, so, the answer to your question is, yes."

Out in the sheriff's office, Clay told Buck he needed a search warrant to go through Lottie's place to hunt for the money she stole from the bank.

Thirty minutes later, armed with a warrant signed by Jason Strong, the man who served as mayor, attorney, and sometimes, judge - Clay, Buck and the judge entered Lottie's saloon. Clay showed the warrant to Amos Tanner who was in charge when Lottie was away.

He wasn't happy about it, but in the face of the sheriff and judge, he had no choice but to let them search the place.

In Lottie's office, they found a safe against the back wall behind her desk. The door was slightly ajar and Clay pulled it open. Behind him, he heard Buck whistle. "Would you look at that? That's more money than I've ever seen at one time."

Tanner stepped up and reached out to close the vault door. "See here, you've got no right to…"

That was as far as he got before Clay grabbed his wrist in a vice like grip. "All I'll be takin' is what she stole from the Fort Smith bank."

Tanner jerked his hand back and said, "You have no right to any of that money. How can you prove any of it actually came from a bank in Fort Smith?"

Clay grinned. "Don't have to. I have a receipt that says she and her gang took thirteen thousand dollars out of the bank back in Fort Smith. I plan on countin' out that amount of money and leave the rest.

Tanner did some quick thinking and said, "Then you'll be committing robbery. That money belongs to me. Miss Simmons has been holding it for me. I don't trust banks."

Before Clay had a chance to retaliate, the judge looked over at Tanner and said, "And I suppose you have a signed receipt?"

Tanner's face turned the color of cotton for just a moment before he regained his composure. "Why no, we had an understanding. She allowed me to keep my money in her safe so it would be available in case I needed it to cover bets. In fact, I was just coming in to get it. I'm thinking of relocating to Chicago. Now, if you don't mind," he said moving toward the safe, again.

Clay stepped in front of him and placed his hand on the butt of his pistol. "Unless you have a signed receipt stating this money belongs to you, then I'm going to deduct what I believe to be the bank's money and you can deal with the judge for whatever is left."

Tanner turned to the judge and asked, "Can he do that?"

"He can, and with my approval," the judge said.

"So, I guess I'll have to be satisfied with what's left," Tanner said, a small glimmer in his eyes.

"Not so fast, Mister Tanner," the judge said. "Whatever is left goes into my safe until this whole thing gets straightened out. You'll have thirty days to prove that money belongs to you. And if you can't, the money goes into probate."

Tanner looked dejected and said, "You're all a bunch of crooks."

Clay laughed and said, "That's like the pot callin' the kettle black."

"What if someone wins a big hand, how am I supposed to pay them off?" Tanner asked.

"Oh, I don't think you'll have that problem," the sheriff said. "As of now, this place is closed."

"You can't do that! What am I supposed to do for a job?" Tanner yelled.

"I guess you can always go to Chicago like you said you plan on doing," Buck said with a grin. "You've got one hour to get your belongings and be out of here. Once I put a padlock on the door, anything that's left belongs to the state."

Back at the sheriff's office, after Clay took out what was due the Fort Smith bank. Buck handed the judge a little over thirty-two thousand dollars. "I think this will go a long way in helping the city make some improvements," he said with a grin.

Clay bought two tickets for Fort Smith and made arrangements for his horse to be loaded onto the train since it would be leaving in less than two hours.

He said his goodbyes and thanked them for their help, then collected his prisoner and boarded the train just minutes before it left the station.

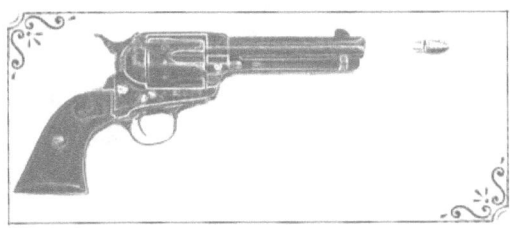

CHAPTER TEN

Earlier, prior to Clay arriving in Memphis, Loralie boarded the train for Knoxville, with smiles and hat tipping from several men. Loralie had changed back into her dress and fixed her hair. No use advertising she was coming back. It was unlikely they would recognize her all gussied up, which is the way she wanted it. Her business was best left unannounced. As the train pulled away, she hoped there would be no train robbers this time; she would have problems enough to face once she got back.

As she hoped for, the trip was uneventful and she lost herself in the passing landscape; even took a nap.

Knoxville was clambering with people, many who were still arguing about the war. The city was divided, half wanting succession the other half against succession. But even so, the city was becoming a booming center for manufacturing; textile and iron works vying for top honors.

The sooner she could get on the trail for Cinch Mountain, the better she would like it; but due to the lateness of the day, she would spend the night in one of the nice hotels with soft beds. It would be the last one she'd sleep in until she could get her house built and have a bed of her own brought in. Before going to the hotel, she would see to boarding her horse.

At the livery stable, the man couldn't believe this beautiful young woman, dressed in a flowery dress, pretty green eyes and flaming red hair, would be wanting to board a horse like the big Morgan; maybe a horse that pulled a buckboard, but not a blooded stallion that most men he knew of, would have trouble controllin'.

When she spoke, he became even more confused.

"Jest want ta board him overnight. We'll be hittin' the trail bright n early in the mornin', so he'll be ah needin' some grain and ah good rubdown."

She looked like a lady, but sounded like a mountain girl. "You look like you come from one of them big cities up north, but sound like somebody from here abouts. Which is it, girl?"

Loralie looked down at the wrinkled old man who didn't look like he weighed enough ta stand up straight in ah strong wind. "Benson, Loralie Benson if'n it's any o' yer concern."

The old man spat a stream of brown tobacco juice at a grasshopper sitting nearby and covered the poor critter with the sticky stuff. "Any relation ta Silas Benson?" he asked.

"He was my pa," Loralie said with sadness in her voice.

"Ya don't say. You that lil freckled faced redhead thet used ta hide behind his pants leg, afraid of her own shadder?"

Loralie smiled, remembering comin' ta town with her pa and hidin' behind him when folks spoke ta her.

"That was ah fer piece back, old man. Now, are you gonna board my horse or do I hav'ta do it my own self?"

Ignoring Loralie's words, the old man looked at the big Morgan and said, "Thought I recognized thet horse. It were yer pa's."

"That's right, it was pa's, and now he's mine. Now, for the last time, you gonna do for him or am I?"

The old man took the reins from her and said, "Be ah dollar. I'll do right by him, and by the way, yer pa was friendlier. What time you gonna come by in the morning?"

Loralie handed him a dollar and said, "I plan on bein' on the road by around six or so. And I'm not unfriendly, just got ah lot on my mind right now."

The old man nodded his head, thinking, nobody wants ta jaw anymore. "He'll be ready."

This time she had no problem getting a room because she looked like a lady, and after leaving her satchel in her room, she went shopping, again; this time for clothes more suitable for riding and hunting and living in the woods while her new house was being built.

After taking her packages to her room, which was the biggest and best she'd ever been in, she took a long, hot bath, then put her dress back on and went down to the restaurant for supper.

This time she wasn't looking for anything fancy. She needed real food and ordered ah big steak with all the trimmings and black coffee.

While she waited for her supper to arrive, she sipped on the strong, black coffee, and looked around. The room was filled with people dressed to the nines, the men in suits and the women in the latest fashion.

While glancing around, she noticed a newspaper on the empty table next to her. She reached across the short distance and retrieved it. It was a Knoxville Gazette, a paper she was familiar with, but it was the front-page story that got her attention.

MULLIN FAMILY TO OPEN A NEW
LUMBER MILL UP ON CINCH MOUNTAIN

A knot formed in Loralie's stomach and for a minute she had trouble breathing. As she read on, the story said the Mullins had filed on the Benson property due to Mr. and Mrs. Benson being killed by Indians and the remaining heirs abandoning the land and leaving the state, leaving no forwarding address.

This was the same malarkey she had read on the poster back in Memphis provided by her father's friend, Price Woodard. By the time she finished reading the article, she was mad enough to bite a ten-penny nail in two with her bare teeth. It was all she could do to eat her supper. How could the sheriff have let this happen? He knew she'd be coming back and had promised ta keep an eye on the place for her. Why hadn't he done something? Why hadn't he stopped them?

Her mind was so filled with questions and anger she had a hard time sleeping. When the restaurant opened up for breakfast, she was dressed in a pair of men's Levis pants, boots, a checkered, flannel work shirt and wore a wide brimmed hat that would shade her face. Her pistol and holster were in her saddlebags, along with her dress and other purchases except for her new Mackinaw coat, which she would tie behind her saddle.

She left her gear at the livery, and then went to the small café. The sign over the door read, "Bonner Café, food for the workingman."

The interior was clean as a hospital room and the smell of bacon was enticing. She'd planned on coffee only, wanting ta get on the road, but she knew she had to control her anger. Going off without something in her belly was not in her best interest. She needed energy for the fight that was soon to come.

The lady that ran the place was in her fifties. She still had a good figure and her eyes were bright and shiny. There were a few traces of gray beginning ta show along her temples, but other than that, she was ah fetching woman. She was dressed in a wide flowing skirt and had on a white shirt that was hidden behind the red apron she wore.

The place was already crowded with men in work clothes. She figured most of them worked at one of the textile plants.

She found a stool at the counter and looked at the menu painted on the wall behind the counter while she waited for the woman to come by and take her order.

In less than thirty seconds, a cup of coffee was placed in front of her. The woman smiled and said, "Hi, I'm Sonya, owner of this establishment. What'll ya have?"

When Loralie looked up at her, the woman stepped back and said, "You're Loralie Benson!"

Loralie looked at the woman and said, "Last time I checked. Do we know each other?"

"You probably don't remember me, I'm Sonya Bonner, formally Sonya Crider, friend of your ma. I'm so sorry to hear of their passin'. Indians, they said."

After studying the woman more closely, she vaguely remembered a younger version coming to the house ah time or two. "Seems I do recollect ah woman that resembles you comin' by the house back when I was ah young'un."

While Loralie ate, Sonya kept pace with her customers, and in between times, Loralie brought Sonya up ta date. When she finished, Sonya put her hands on her hips and said through clenched teeth, "Them Mullins have never been anythin' but trouble since they first come ta Cinch Mountain."

"Well, when I get finished with'm they'll be wishin' they hadn't never come ta the mountain in the first place. If'n they won't leave peaceful like, I guarantee they won't be causin' trouble fer nobody else, lessen' they can climb out from under six feet o' dirt," Loralie said with conviction.

"You'd best be careful. Ole man Mullin ain't particular when it comes ta females or who he shoots in the back," Sonya advised.

When Loralie went to pay her bill, she found a package waiting for her. "Just ah little somethin' fer the road," Sonya said with a big smile. "And you remember what I said bout ole man Mullin, you hear?"

Loralie thanked her and went to the livery where she bought another horse, a three-year-old appaloosa mare. During breakfast she'd decided to stop by the mercantile store for supplies before she headed up the mountain. The way things were looking; she would need plenty of grub and ammunition in case she had to hole up for a spell.

While loading her supplies, she wondered what kind of problems she'd run into when she got back? She doubted she would she get any help from the sheriff. They most likely promised him money from the sale of the timber to look the other way.

Glancing over her shoulder, she saw the telegraph sign down at the railroad office and wondered if she should send ah wire, asking for the ranger's help, even though it was technically out of his jurisdiction.

She laughed and spoke to herself, "Loralie Benson, if you ain't the silliest woman in the world, thinkin' bout askin' fer help from ah man you hardly know. By now, he probably don't even remember yer name and he's probably already on his way, takin' that Lottie woman back ta Fort Smith ta stand trial. Sides, you shouldn't need any help ta run off ah few Mullins. If'n things get too tough, you can always call on cousin Lacy down in White River, Kentucky. She's hell on wheels when it comes to ah shootout and I'll bet she'd come ah runnin' jest fer the excitement of it. Plus, there's them Hackers. They'd be willin' ta help, I'm bettin'. "

By eight o'clock that morning, Loralie was astride the big Morgan with the appaloosa trailing behind. She was headed north toward Cinch Mountain and the dance she was about to open.

A few miles north of Knoxville, she pulled her horse to a stop and stood up in the stirrups, looking at the blue Tennessee sky. In the far horizon, she could see the tops of several mountains were covered in fog. Memories of her childhood flooded her mind, but when one of the images changed to her ma and pa laying in the yard, dead, tears came into her eyes. She sat back down on the saddle and urged the big Morgan on, wiping tears from her eyes that were replaced with anger and a yearning for revenge.

That night she camped alongside a small stream and made a smokeless fire from dried twigs she'd found inside the tree line. The night was getting cold, but she dared not to have a big fire. While she got along with most of the Cherokee up around her place, this was not yet Cinch Mountain and she knew there were hostiles about. She'd seen sign here and there; mainly unshod hoof prints. The Indians were masters of leaving no sign when they didn't want to be found. But this part of Tennessee was

Cherokee country for the most part and they did mostly what they pleased, including raiding.

She made her bed on a pile of pine boughs, covered over with a piece of canvas, close to the fire to get all the warmth she could.

After staring at the stars for quite some time, she finally drifted off and dreamed of the big white house she intended on building. She was sitting on the wide front porch, dressed in ah bright red dress with white bows on it. She was sipping on something in a real glass. The sun was just going down over the tops of the trees when all at once she heard wild screaming and looked up and saw a bunch of men with masks on their faces come ah riding hell bent for leather into the yard. They had torches and tossed them through the windows of her beautiful new home and into the barn. One of them started shooting all of her horses.

She jumped up to get her rifle when one of them came riding right up to the porch. He raised his rifle and pointed directly at her. She saw flame shoot out of the end of the barrel and heard the loud boom.

Loralie sat up, wild eyed and trembling. Her breathing was coming in ragged gasps. She looked around and saw that she was still at her small camp near the stream. She gave a sigh of relief and got up, adding more sticks to the hot embers. She looked at the sky and judged the time to be close to four in the morning; time to get up and get around. It would be daylight soon and she wanted to be headed north by then.

She put the coffee pot on to boil water, then brushed down the backs of her two horses to warm them up some before putting the saddle and packs on them, otherwise they could get a mite temperamental. By the time she was done, the coffee was boiling and she pulled some jerky from one of the packs and had a quick breakfast. She was still a bit shaken from her dream.

As she swung her leg over the big Morgan, she vowed from this point on, to never be farther than an arm's reach from a gun of some kind.

All that day she turned things over in her mind about how she was going to deal with the situation at home. She wondered if they'd thrown a log cabin together and was livin' on the property. If they had, what would she do then?

Would she need a lawyer? She didn't even know if there was such a thing anywhere nearby. And if there was, how would she go about hiring him? She didn't even have a deed to the property. She reckoned it was burned when they fired the house. So how was she to prove the place belonged ta her? She couldn't just go in and start shootin'. She'd probably wind up being the first woman in Tennessee to get herself hung.

That night at her campsite, she was drinking coffee while leaning with her back against a spruce tree when a thought struck her. What if she could get them to start the ruckus? That way she'd just be defending herself. For just a moment she was excited by the idea, then she realized she had absolutely no idea on how to go about doing that.

Frustrated with grief at the thought that she'd never be able ta get her land back, Loralie had no appetite and rolled up in her blankets and tried to go to sleep. She needed to get home. Only then would she be able ta size up the situation and make some plans.

Loralie was looking at the stars when out of the corner of her eye she saw the big Morgan's head come up, then the appaloosas.

As quickly and quietly as she could, she rolled out of her blankets, grabbed her rifle and disappeared into the forest. She'd no more than raised her rifle to her shoulder than she heard a man's voice.

"Loralie Benson, you put thet rifle down. You ain't plannin' on shootin' ah friend are ya?"

Loralie sighed and lowered the rifle, then walked back into her campsite. "John D. Hacker, you shouldn't be sneakin' up on ah poor defenseless girl, like that."

John D. Hacker walked into the light of the fire, slapping his leg and gee-hawfing, "Poor defenseless girl my foot. Sneakin' up on you is like tryin' ta sneak up on ah rattlesnake."

He had a deer across his shoulders and tossed it on the ground near the fire.

"How'd you know I was here?" she asked.

"Saw ya earlier taday from up on the hill, yonder," he said pointing up the mountainside. "Figured this might be where you'd lite fer the night, sos I come by ta say welcome back and share some deer meat with ya. That is, if'n you ain't lost yer taste for deer meat?"

While John D. was cutting off a couple of deer steaks, Loralie built up the fire.

Over coffee, deer meat, and a few wild onions Loralie had picked earlier, but hadn't eaten, John D. brought her up ta date about her land and what he had to say wasn't good.

CHAPTER ELEVEN

Lottie Simmons stared out of the train car window. She was shackled hand and feet. The hatred she felt for Clay Brentwood showed in her eyes. The only good part was when people walked by and stared at her all trussed up in irons. They would remember her alright and one day when she was bigger than Belle Starr, they would remember seeing her.

She didn't know how or when, but she would escape, and when she did, there would be a dead ranger left behind.

Lottie knew the gun hands that worked for her at the saloon were in jail and couldn't do much, but they hadn't taken into account her other contacts that would lose money if she were to be locked away in prison. First, there was Amos Tanner. Tanner was one of the slickest dealers she'd ever seen and skimmed money from the patrons; not much from each one, but over the course of the night, he did well, plus making a lot of money for the house. If her place was to close down, Amos would lose a sweet deal.

Then there was Emil Brewster, the man she bought whiskey from – stolen whiskey at a bargain price, along with a big profit for Emil. Being his biggest customer and friends with Amos, they would not like Lottie's place to close down. They would more than likely go see Grant Mousier, her attorney. Between the three of them, they would figure something out. She might even have to go into hiding for awhile. Grant could draw up false papers, saying she'd sold the place to him. In the meantime, she would be free to rob a great many banks. And when her reputation got big enough, she would have enough money to retire to someplace like, Europe or maybe South America and live like a queen.

Even though Lottie was shackled and couldn't move very fast, Clay was feeling on edge and his eyes never missed a movement inside the train car. The man sitting a few seats in front of them, on the opposite side seemed to be paying a lot of attention to them. He was dressed in a business suit and wore a flat, western style hat. The man looked like a banker or an attorney, but looks can be deceiving. Thinking back, Clay remembered the man who pretended to be a drummer, but in reality was an assassin intent on murdering him. Only sheer luck had saved him that time.

The man stood up and walked out onto the train car landing. Clay watched through the glass window as the man retrieved a cigar from his inside coat pocket, and lit it.

Clay looked through the windows on both sides of the train to see if that had been a signal, but saw no one riding alongside the train, trying to board. He leaned back in his seat and drew a deep breath. He was just being overly cautious. The man was probably just what he appeared to be. To be on the safe side, Clay glanced over in Lottie's direction to see if she was reacting to the man, but there was no change in her as she glared at him.

Clay relaxed and leaned back in his seat, feeling foolish for being as skittish as a newborn colt. He would take Lottie back to Fort Smith, turn her over to the sheriff and that would be the end of it. A few weeks from now he would be home, making plans to rebuild his own place. He guessed he would need to hire some hands.

Clay had just reached up and pulled his hat down over his eyes, thinking to get some rest, when he felt the end of a pistol barrel being pressed against the back of his head and heard a woman's voice, saying, "Raise both of your hands up and place them behind your head like you're resting, and I won't have to shoot you, Mister Brentwood."

At that point, the young woman sitting across the aisle from him stood up and stepped over and went through Clay's vest pockets, retrieving the key for the locks on Lottie's shackles.

Clay stared at her, wondering why he hadn't noticed her before. She was dressed like a dancehall girl and wore heavy makeup.

Lottie looked over and smiled. This was even faster than she'd hoped for.

Once Lottie was free, she stood over Clay and looked down at him, a snarl on her mouth. She balled up her fist and hit him square in the face, then smiled and said, "That was just a sample of what you're going to get before you die, Mister Texas Ranger. You thought you were so smart; you and that little floozy, Loralie Benson. Well, I'm here to tell you, both of you are going to die a long, slow, death."

By now, three more women were up and pointing guns at the other passengers. The man in the suit came back inside and walked up to Lottie and said, "Name's Daniel Smart, I'm a friend of Grant Mousier. He hired me to make sure you and the ranger didn't make it back to Fort Smith."

As Daniel and Lottie went off, talking, the women locked Clay up with his own shackles. Feeling like an idiot wouldn't come close to the way he felt.

One of the women bent down and touched her finger to the tip of his nose and said, "Maybe she'll let us have some fun with you before she kills you. Would you like that, Mister Ranger Man?"

The other women laughed and poked her on the arm. Clay stared straight ahead, trying to think of some way out of this situation. Loralie had left for Kentucky before he headed the opposite direction with Lottie, so she would be hard to track down. She was safe for now, leaving him free to think about the problem at hand, escaping and taking Lottie into custody again, and getting her to Fort Smith.

The train began to slow down and finally came to a stop not more than five miles west of Memphis. The train had topped over a small rise and could not be seen from town. Three cowboys got off the train, lowered the ramp and began unloading nine saddled horses, including Clay's black stallion.

One of the women guarding Clay, nudged him in the shoulder and said, "We had a man riding with the engineer to make sure he stopped the train where we wanted him to, so we can get off. That Daniel Smart, he thinks of everything."

Outside, they had to take the shackles off Clay's ankles so he could ride and as he swung a leg over the saddle, he was tempted to make a run for it, but changed his mind. He had no food, no water and no weapon. He was sure the black stallion could out run them the short distance back to Memphis, but they would probably shoot his horse out from under him before he got twenty yards. Lottie had his saddlebags, which had an extra pistol, and ammunition – along with five hundred dollars cash money.

As they rode north, away from the train, Clay glanced over his shoulder and saw the train beginning to move in reverse, and grinned. The engineer was going back to Memphis to report what had happened. Maybe the sheriff would form a posse and come looking, or maybe not.

CHAPTER TWELVE

With John D. rolled up in his soogun on the opposite side of the fire, Loralie was able to relax a little. She was still keyed up, but as John D. has stated, "Ain't nothin' you can do 'til you get home and size up the situation, so why cause yourself more grief than you half'ta."

He was right, of course, so with some effort, she was able to clear her mind somewhat and finally drift off into a deep sleep.

She dreamed of a big white house and a red barn with white corral fences. There was a garden out back and roses growing in front of the house. She was sitting on the front porch in a big rocking chair; enjoying the cool; clear evening as the sun dropped off to the west. She was content with the world. Suddenly she heard the sound of horses running. Then, seemingly out of nowhere, the Mullins came chargin' into the yard, guns blazin' and ole man Mullins hisself rode right up to the porch and aimed his pistol at her and fired.

Loralie sat straight up, screaming, "Nooooo!"

John D. Hacker was out of his soogun, pistol in hand, looking for someone to shoot, but all he saw was Loralie sitting on her bedroll, eyes wide and wild looking.

He walked over and asked, "You alright?"

"Of course, I'm alright," she spat at him. "Had ah bad dream, that's all."

John D. looked at her for a moment; squatted next to the fire adding a few sticks and then filled the coffee pot with water and sat it on the flat rock sitting in the edge of the fire. When it began to boil, he would add the makin's.

Without looking over his shoulder he asked, "Them Mullins got you ah mite stirred up, do they?"

"How'd you know that?" Loralie asked, a puzzled look on her face.

"Person has enemies, they're bound ta have ah nightmare or two."

"You ever have one? Ah nightmare?" Loralie asked as she got to her feet and walked over next to the fire.

"Couple ah times, as ah matter of fact," John D. said as he dumped coffee grounds into the boiling water. "Mainly about a Cherokee they called, Adahy. Means lives in the woods. We was at war with the Cherokee then and he was considered big medicine. In my dream he would come out of the trees like a ghost and draw his bow and shoot an arrow at me while I was sleepin'. Scared the be-Jesus out of me I'm here ta tell ya. Had me ah time sleepin'. Finally, ah few years later, after we'd come ta terms with'm, I met him face ta face. He was just ah frail old man who could hardly get around. I told him about my dreams and he just smiled and nodded his head."

"We were enemies then," he said. "But I am old now. You have no need to fear me, it is a warrior called Horse who is still at war with the whites."

"I never met this, Horse, and I've never had any night dreams about him, either. Heard he was killed over on the other side of the mountain. Once you get home and find out what the score is, you'll be ok. It's the unknown that scares us."

Loralie told John D. about her recurring dream as he poured them both fresh coffee.

John D. blew on the steaming brew, then took a sip. "If'n I was ta comment on it, I would say it was ah warnin' ta sleep with yer rifle close by and one eye open."

Loralie looked at the sky and saw lightness in the east. She sliced some bacon into a skillet and sat it on a rock in the middle of the fire. Next, she got some biscuits from her tack and sat them in two tin plates. It wasn't much, but on the trail, you don't expect a seven course meal.

"I'll be headin' off toward my place when we leave here," John D. said, as he stuffed a piece of biscuit and bacon in his mouth. "That is unless you think you can't handle things by yerself."

Loralie looked at John D. and said, "Ain't never seen the day when I can't handle them Mullins, thout no help from ah Hacker."

"Kinda what I figured," John D. said with a grin. "But if'n you get yerself outnumbered, you send word and me and my kin will come ah runnin'. Ain't never had no truck with them Mullins, no-how."

"Shucks," Loralie said. "Kinda figured that all along, and I'll shore keep it in mind if'n there be more'n ten of 'em."

After breakfast, they parted ways, Loralie heading straight north and John D. off to the northwest.

The big Morgan must have known where they were headed because he pulled at the bit and wanted to run. Loralie loosened the reins and let him have his head for a couple of miles before pulling him back to a ground-eating lope. The appaloosa had also enjoyed the run. No use wearing them out, she would be home by noontime tomorrow and the trouble that was for sure, waiting on her.

CHAPTER THIRTEEN

Leading the way, Lottie and Daniel skirted Memphis to the north. Lottie was laughing at something Daniel had said. The three cowboys and the three women rode in pairs on each side of him and one pair behind. Clay noticed they stayed as much as they could to the trees so they wouldn't be seen, which was easy since this part of Tennessee was fairly flat with lots of trees. They crossed a small tributary feeding off the Mississippi that ran through Memphis.

As they came out of the river, Clay noticed that this part of Tennessee was lush with a wide variety of trees. So far, he'd seen hickory, two species of ash, silver maple and two species of mulberry. He remembered sitting in a mulberry tree as a boy, stuffing his face with mulberries and having the stain on his face and hands for days to come.

He also saw poison ivy growing in abundance, which he tried to stay clear of, wondering if he could somehow use it to help him escape? Probably not, but he would keep it in the back of his mind.

It was late afternoon when they rode out of a stand of trees and stopped. In front of them was a wide valley that housed what looked to be a well-rounded farm. He could see a cornfield, a patch of tobacco, and beyond that was a hayfield. Off to the right were both, beef cattle and a combination of riding horses, workhorses and mules. The house was a large two-story, painted white. There was a wide front porch and the ground in front of it was covered with grass. There were several outbuildings, including a smoke house for curing meat. The barn was very large and painted red. Out behind the house, he could see the edge of what looked to be a garden. And between the house and the barn was what looked to be a bunkhouse. Clay could see at least ten men working at various jobs.

"Well, here we are, Lottie, your new home for awhile," Daniel said, sweeping his hand in a wide arc.

Lottie stared across the farm then turned her head toward Daniel. "Who owns this place and where will I be staying? And how will I be able to run my affairs from here? Will I be able to come and go as I please, or am I to be a captive?"

"Whoa!" Daniel said, raising his hands palms forward. "One question at a time. "The owner of this fine farm is none other than your attorney, Grant Mousier, so it will be safe for you to stay here for a while. As far as the other questions go, you'll have to take that up with him, but I'm sure he has a plan."

Lottie stared at him for a moment, then turned her horse and headed in the direction of the farmhouse.

Since they had no jail, Clay was shoved roughly into the smokehouse for the time being. There was no meat being cured at the present, which left Clay plenty of room to roam around. The building was solid, made from hickory with rows of maple slats for hanging meat on both sides of a center aisle. There was a wood-burning stove at one end, but even if he pulled the smokestack apart, the hole was too small for him to climb through. It was very dark inside with little light with which to move around, so for the time being, he hunkered down next to the door to try and listen to what was going on outside. Other than the regular hands coming and going he learned nothing. He sat his saddlebags next to him, knowing they had taken his extra pistol and ammunition. Thinking he had no weapons after taking his waist gun and rifle, he had not been searched further. He lowered his hand to the top of the right boot and felt inside. The knife he carried there was resting in its hiding place, waiting for the right moment.

Grant Mousier was there to greet them, telling her he was glad to see her and not to worry; he had things worked out. Lottie would have the whole upstairs as her apartment. Of course, she would come down for meals and had free run of the place. While he didn't say she couldn't leave, he strongly advised her to sit tight for a while, at least until things quieted down. The sheriff would have a posse out looking for her, but he doubted they would come here.

Lottie's head was in a bit of a daze. She never realized Mousier had a place like this. It was a nice setup and no matter what, he would be sitting pretty. Well, why not, Lottie thought, after all he is an attorney, along with being good looking and smart. Hadn't he gotten her out of several scrapes, including the one he'd just gotten her out of. It must have cost him a pretty penny.

Later, after supper, they were sitting in his downstairs office with its big mahogany desk and soft, leather chair. Lottie was sitting on a couch to one side of the room, sipping on a very good cognac.

"This is a very nice setup you have here, Grant," Lottie said as she accepted the tailor made cigarette he offered her from a hand engraved, cherry wood cigarette box. "Very nice indeed."

"It should be," Grant said with a chuckle. "You helped pay for it."

Lottie wasn't sure how she felt about that, but finally conceded that he had been worth ever cent she'd paid him to keep her out of jail. "And just how much has it cost me so far for this little escapade?" she asked with a smile, wondering how much he'd paid Daniel and his people to snatch her from the ranger.

Grant Mousier lit a cigar and blew out a smoke ring before answering her. "Not a cent, yet. I figured you'd like to pay him yourself."

Lottie smiled, knowing now how he was able to afford this place. He spent very little of his own money, except on himself. Oh, he was smart, all right. "And did he tell you an amount, a fee for him and his people?"

"He did, and I accepted on your behalf because I knew if anyone could do it, he could."

Lottie was beginning to get impatient. "Ok, if we're through dancing around the bush, I'd like to know how much I owe and when does he expect to get paid?"

Grant took a sip of his cognac, then set the sniffer on his desk. "Ten thousand to Daniel and he pays his own people. My bill comes to two thousand for setting it up."

"That's twelve thousand dollars!" Lottie screamed.

"Well, the lady can add," Grant said after taking another sip.

"And when does he expect to get paid?" Lottie said, sitting up a bit straighter.

"Today," Grant said, matter of factly.

"And you think I have that kind of money on me?" she asked.

"I do." Grant said. "It is my understanding that the ranger took thirteen thousand out of your safe to give back to the bank in Fort Smith. He said that was how much you stole. Daniel and I agree, you can pay us out of that money and still have a thousand dollars cash walking around money."

Lottie was unaware that Clay had taken money from her safe to pay it back to the bank, but relieved she would have enough money on hand to pay them off and still have some cash left. What happened to the rest of the money in her office safe?

As best as she could remember there should still be over twenty thousand dollars. Was it still there or did Amos Tanner take it and skip out on her? She wouldn't put it past him. And what about the money she had in the city bank? There was over forty thousand dollars in her private account. They couldn't take that, too, could they?

Twelve thousand dollars seemed to be a lot of money to pay for getting her off the train and out of the clutches of the law, but only a drop in the bucket to what she would make being free to rob other banks; plus, she still had her saloon, even though she couldn't show her face in Memphis, at least for awhile.

Grant brought her out of her thoughts with his next statement. "You know the mayor is planning on saying you abandoned the saloon and therefore, claiming it for the city of Memphis. After six months, he will sell it to the sheriff for a pittance of what it's worth, with the proviso that the sheriff shares the profits with the city. This will all be an under the table deal. The city will be what is called, a silent partner."

"They can't do that, can they?" Lottie asked, flabbergasted at the thought.

"They can and they will, unless…"

"Unless what?" Lottie asked, sitting up a little straighter in her chair.

"Unless we can show paper that says I am an investor and silent partner in the saloon," Grant said, blowing another smoke ring into the air over her head.

"And just how do we accomplish that little feat? You do know that the mayor is also the judge who probably thought up this whole affair in case they were able to close me down," Lottie said, looking Grant straight in the eyes.

"Yes, I am well aware of that," Grant said with a sly smile on his face. "I happen to be close friends with a judge up in the capital, who for a fee, will make the records show I have been a silent partner from the beginning."

Grant leaned back in his chair and drained his glass of cognac, then asked, "So, what do you think? As far as the people of Memphis know, as a part owner, I'll be running the saloon in your absence and you'll be free to indulge yourself in whatever other money making endeavors that suit you fancy."

Lottie felt like she was being manipulated but what could she do? Reluctantly, she nodded her head.

"Fine. I'll write up the paperwork for you to sign," Grant said with a look of satisfaction. "Now, about the money to pay Daniel?"

Lottie was cognizant of the fact that he hadn't included himself in the statement, but she also knew he meant he wanted his money too.

Clay had just come down from the rafters where he'd been looking for a way out of the smokehouse, but had come up empty. When the door opened, Lottie saw Clay sitting on the floor, his saddlebags a few feet away. She stepped inside and immediately walked over and picked up the saddlebags and began rummaging through them. She dumped the contents on the floor. There was a razor, a bar of soap, a towel, a change of clothes and some beef jerky, and a measly five hundred dollars.

She threw the saddlebags onto the floor and looked at Clay. "Where is it?" she asked, placing her hands on her hips.

"Where is what?" Clay asked without looking up. "You know what," Lottie screamed. "Where is my money? I know you stole thirteen thousand dollars out of my private safe."

"Oh, that money," Clay said, nodding his head. "I don't have it."

"What do you mean you don't have it?" Lottie asked, confusion on her face.

Clay stood up. "Which part of that sentence didn't you understand? I do not have the money," he said slowly as though he was speaking to an illiterate. "Tanner said it was his and you were just holdin' it for him."

Lottie looked at Grant. "He's lying. Tanner would never have said that except to maybe try and protect my money."

Turning back to Clay she asked, "And did you give it to him?"

"The answer to that would be, no. None of us believed him."

"So, you do have my money?" Lottie said, getting tired of this little run around game Clay was playing.

"Like I said before, No, I don't have that money."

By now, Daniel Smart and several of Grant's men had eased up, curious as to what was going on.

Grant drew his pistol and pointed it at Clay, then nodded to one of his men. "Search the place."

They all stood by while the man searched the room. Finally, he approached Grant and said, "It's not here, boss. Maybe he has it on him."

Grant called for two more of his men, then told the three of them, "Search him!"

Clay looked at Grant. "Are you as dumb as she is? I said I don't have that money on me, nor do I have it hidden somewhere."

"Then where is it?" Lottie asked, running out of patience.

"Probably back in the bank in Fort Smith by now, would be my guess."

"And just how did you accomplish that little feat, send it by carrier pigeon?" Lottie asked.

"Somethin' like that," Clay said. "I turned it over to the bank in Memphis and they wired the money back to the bank in Fort Smith. I ain't stupid enough ta walk around with that kind of money on me… too much temptation for people like you."

"You're lying," Lottie said. She turned to Grant. "Have your men work him over until he tells us where the money is".

Deep inside, Lottie wanted the pleasure of killing him, herself, very slowly, but first things first.

Grant nodded at three men standing close by. The tallest one, a man with a long, lanky, hard muscled frame, smashed Clay in the face with his fist before Clay had a chance to duck.

Being pinned against the wall, Clay had no room to maneuver and when he raised his left arm to block a second punch, the man on his right drove his fist into Clay's kidney, causing him a great deal of pain.

The third man hit Clay so hard on the left side of his head, he almost passed out.

Clay knew he had to do something or they might beat him to death, or near it to get information out of him. They wouldn't believe the truth if it was written on paper and signed by a judge.

Clay saw a fist coming at him from the man in front of him and ducked straight down. The man's fist hit the wall as Clay put his right foot against the wall and pushed off, driving his shoulder into the stomach of the man in front of him. The man let out a rush of air and staggered backward.

With speed they hadn't expected, Clay reached out and grabbed the barrel of the pistol in Grant's hand and gave a jerk, then flipped it around so that it now rested in his hand. He pointed the pistol at Grant and said, "Call'm off or you'll be the first to die."

Daniel Smart, standing just off to the side went for his pistol and had just cleared leather when the bullet from Clay's pistol knocked him backward. A small hole in his forehead was seeping blood.

It happened so fast no one else had a chance to react before Clay pointed the pistol back in Grant's direction. "Tell'm ta back off or you're ah dead man," Clay said with conviction.

"Hold it!" Grant yelled, sweat breaking out on his forehead. He was fine as long as he was in control, but he wasn't about to die because of Lottie or any other woman.

"Everbody unshuck your guns and toss'm out in the yard," Clay said motioning toward the door. When everyone had done as they were told, Clay looked at Lottie and said, "Put my things back in my saddlebags and then step over here next to me."

"And if I refuse?" Lottie asked, placing her hands on her hips in defiance.

"I do my best to never shoot a lady, but since I don't consider you a lady, I reckon I'll just have ta shoot ya. My warrant says, dead or alive."

"You wouldn't dare," Lottie challenged.

"You've got to the count of three. One…"

Lottie squatted down and did as she was told. The look in Clay's eyes told her he wasn't bluffing.

Outside, Clay had just dropped the lock into the hasp and snapped it shut when two men came out of the bunkhouse. They saw Lottie and Clay and began running toward them.

"A thousand dollars to the man who kills this man," Lottie yelled, pointing her finger at Clay.

The two men, confused about what to do, came to a stop.

Clay pointed his pistol at Lottie and said, "Be kinda hard ta collect from a dead woman. Either one of you slaps leather, she dies."

Both men stood very quiet, not making a move, undecided what to do next.

"Unbuckle them gun belts and toss'm over next to the horses, then lie face down in the yard with your arms spread wide and don't move," Clay said with authority.

Fortunately, all of the horses were still standing at the railing in front of the house and when Clay and Lottie approached, the black stallion whinnied and shook its head up and down.

To his surprise, his handgun and holster were hanging from the saddle horn. Clay would put it on later, after they were away from here.

Next, he made Lottie stand with her arms around one of the pillars at the edge of the porch and warned her not to move.

Even though she did what he said, the look in her eyes was pure hatred. "You won't get away with this," she said as she wrapped her arms around the pillar.

Clay ignored her as he went about taking his lariat from his saddle and tying the other horses in a string, then swung aboard the black stallion. Pointing his pistol at Lottie, he ordered her to get aboard the horse right behind the black stallion, and when she did as he asked, he headed back toward Memphis at a gallop with Lottie and the other horses trailing along behind.

The smoke house was not meant to be a jail, so it didn't take too many times of the men inside ramming it with their shoulders to knock the door off its hinges. As they poured out into the yard, they saw Clay and Lottie racing toward a line of trees in the distance.

Grant raced for the house and came back out onto the porch with a long-range rifle in his hands. He lifted it to his shoulder and looked down the barrel of the telescope until he had Clay's back in the crosshairs. He took a breath and squeezed the trigger.

At that same moment, Lottie decided to try and escape and urged her horse to the side and forward, hoping to knock Clay from the black stallion, and make an escape back to the ranch.

Unfortunately for her, she was directly behind Clay when Grant pulled the trigger and instead of Clay getting shot, the bullet caught Lottie squarely between the shoulder blades.

Clay reacted to the sound of the rifle by slamming his boots against the sides of the black stallion. The big horse leaped into a full out run, with the trailing horses not far behind.

Grant cursed as he watched them disappear into the trees, not knowing whether he'd killed the ranger or not.

Two minutes later, when Clay knew they were in the clear for the time being, he looked back and saw Lottie slumped over, barely staying on the saddle.

He pulled the black stallion to a stop, then jumped down and went to see about Lottie.

There was blood on the back of Lottie's jacket and her breathing was shallow. After securing her to the saddle, he told her, "Hang in there. I'll get you to a doctor in town."

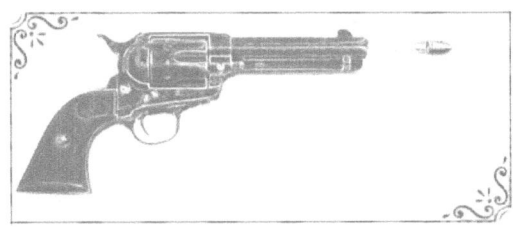

CHAPTER FOURTEEN

It was late afternoon when Loralie Benson eased her horse to a stop, not far from where her home used to be. She had been smelling smoke for some time now. She ground hitched her horses, then eased forward as quietly as she could until she could see the yard.

Three tents were pitched in front of where her parent's house used to be. She counted nine Mullins either sitting in chairs around a large fire pit, or doing other chores. Finally, old man Mullins himself came strutting out of one of the tents and motioned for the others to come to him.

"In ah few days we gonna start cuttin' timber, right here," he said, waving his arms in a circle. "We'll be cuttin' here fer several reasons. First, sos we can build us ah cabin ta live in. I hate these tents. And second, sos we can sell the rest ta make enough money to build us ah sawmill. And when the money starts comin' in, we can build us ah big fancy house down next to the creek. That's an awful purdy spot fer ah house."

Angus, his oldest son, spit a long stream of tobacco juice onto the ground, then asked, "How we gonna sell the lumber if'n we ain't got no saw mill, pa?"

"We trim the limbs off by hand and drag the logs down ta town with mules. Got ah feller down there thet will buy'm. Says he'll cut'm up and sell the pieces ta the town folks what need wood ta burn fer the winter."

Several of the other boys nodded their heads. One of them said, "Pa sure is ah smart'un ain't he? He don't miss ah trick."

Loralie had heard enough and eased back to her horses. She stepped into the stirrup and swung aboard the Morgan. The packhorse followed along behind as they headed up the mountainside. There was a cave she knew of where she could hide without much chance of being discovered. She didn't think the Mullins knew about it. Fact was, as far as she knew; only her and her pa knew it was there. It was sheltered by trees until a person was right up in front of it. A ring of boulders guarded the entrance and the cave couldn't actually be seen until you went through a small passageway between the boulders. The cave itself went back into the mountain nearly a hundred feet and was close to twenty feet wide, giving shelter for both herself and her horses.

That night Loralie had a warm fire going, well back inside the cave, with brush piled up between the fire and the entrance so no one could see the glow. The smoke from the fire was drawn into a crack in the ceiling and went somewhere that couldn't be seen. The horses were bedded down deeper in the back of the cave where water seeped from the rocks into a small pool – not big and not deep, but enough to keep them alive.

Loralie spread her soogun not far from the fire, then sat with her back against the wall, eating some stew she'd put together from the meat and vegetables she'd bought before coming up the mountain. The meat was dried and a mite tough, but it would do until she could set a couple of traps and get some fresh game. She didn't plan on living here for very long, but while she did, she figured to be comfortable.

Long into the night, Loralie's mind searched for ways of stopping the Mullins. In a few days, they would start cutting down her trees and she had to find a way to stop them.

Well before daylight Loralie was putting sticks onto the smoldering hot coals just waiting to be a blazing hot fire again.

Shortly, she was eating more of last night's stew and drinking coffee, going over once more the plan she'd come up with. It probably wouldn't put enough fear into them to cause them to leave, but it sure would slow them down ah bit until she could figure a better plan.

The first thing she had to do was go down to town and get some things she hadn't thought to buy on her way up.

Cinch Mountain wasn't much more than a few stores grouped together to provide for the folks that lived in the vicinity. There was a blacksmith shop that doubled as a livery, The Water'n Hole Saloon, the general store, the sheriff's office, a restaurant and a few other stores. The general store wasn't large, but it was crammed from floor to ceiling with almost anything mountain folks might need, like flour, grain, material for making clothes, saws, axes, guns, ammunition and such.

The owner, Percival Hawks, looked up and then took a double take. "Well bless my hide if it ain't Loralie Benson. We thought you left this part of the country for good. Have you heard what the Mullins done?"

Loralie walked over to the counter and said, "Yes sir, I have, and I'll have you know I never abandoned my land, just went off for ah spell sos I could make some money to rebuild the place. Even told the sheriff, and he said he'd look after things for me, but I reckon his word don't mean much."

"You plan on trying to get your land back?" he asked, excitement in his eyes.

"Yes sir, that's why I'm here, they plan on startin' ta cut in ah few days and I plan on stoppin' them."

Percival looked around and saw no one else in the store, then asked, "You bring help?"

"No sir," Loralie replied, wondering why he'd asked that.

Before she could ask, Percival said, "Maybe you should think on what you're doin', ah mite. Them Mullins got no truck with anyone that ain't with'em and remember, they be mountain folk, born and bred sos they are good trackers and good shots. And they don't get shy about whether it's ah male or female that they shoot at," Percival said shaking his head.

Loralie had known this from the onset, but in her anger, she'd gone against one of her papa's cardinal rules; "Don't never underestimate yer enemy and don't go makin' ah move thout givin' it some deep thinkin'. Remember gal, them that don't abide by that rule, usually wind up never seen er heard from again."

Loralie gave Percival her list and said she would pick it up in a couple of days. Outside, she mounted the big Morgan and turned his head toward Knoxville, the closest place where she might be able to find a lawyer.

It was late in the evening when she rode into Knoxville, tired from the fast pace she'd put the big Morgan through. Although he never showed it, she knew her horse had to be tired, too, as her eyes searched for a livery sign.

She hadn't ridden far when off to her right, down a side street, she found what she was looking for and when she stepped down, a sign on the front door read, 'Gone ta supper, back soon.'

Loralie was of no mind to wait around, so she stripped the saddle and bridle off her horse and gave him a good rubdown with a piece of burlap that was hanging from a peg on the wall of the stall; gave him some oats, fresh hay, and filled the water trough, then left three dollars on the holster's desk.

She saw a restaurant sign just down the street and when she went in, she saw the man who had to be the holster of the livery stable. He was a big, well-muscled man, wearing bib overalls and a shirt with no sleeves. His long, gray hair was pulled back into a ponytail and he had a bushy moustache. He had obviously finished his meal and was enjoying a piece of berry pie. A cup of steaming hot coffee sat nearby.

Loralie walked over and introduced herself and told the man what she had done and asked if three dollars was sufficient?

The man grinned and invited her to join him. "Three dollars is morn' enough. Truth be told, I'd board him for free. You're that Benson gal, ain'tcha'?"

Loralie nodded her head, yes, and before she could continue, the holster went on. "Me and your pappy did some business together. He'd bring in a string of six or seven horses and leave'm with me. I'd sell'm for top dollar, they were that good, make myself ah nice commission, and your papa still made a goodly amount of money. You still got that big Morgan of his?"

"He's the one I got boarded down at your livery barn," Loralie said.

About then the waitress showed up and took Loralie's order, which turned out to be the special of the day – beef stew, with fresh baked bread, butter, pie and coffee for two bits.

When the waitress left, the holster stuck out his hand and said, "Big Hank."

Loralie shook his ham sized paw and was surprised at the gentle handshake.

"Sorry ta hear about yer ma and pa. And even sorrier ta hear them Mullins have taken over the land and gonna cut down all the trees."

"Not if I can help it," Loralie said.

Over supper, she told him the whole story and finally, the reason she was here in town.

The big holster smiled and said, "Musta' been ah good wind that blew you my way. I just happen ta know the sharpest and most honest lawyer there ever was, and he's right here in town. Name's Henry Wadsworth Millstone, named after that writer feller."

Big Hank pulled a pocket watch from inside a place on the front of his overalls, clicked open the lid, looked at the time and put the watch back where it came from. "Too late ta see him today, but first thing in the mornin', after breakfast, we'll go see him. Maybe even see him here. He eats here on ah regular basis."

"And you've known this man for some time?" Loralie asked.

"Since he worked for me at the stable afore goin' off ta law school. Not ah bad smithy, either. Taught him all he knows about that."

Loralie thanked him, paid her bill and went to the hotel. The place had no name, just a sign out front that said, HOTEL.

The room was clean and neat. Nothing fancy, but there was a tub and she ordered hot water and took a bath.

The following morning, she walked into the restaurant and knew something was wrong. Big Hank was sitting at a table, his head bent down and looking like his best huntin' dog had died.

"No luck with yer lawyer friend?" Loralie asked.

Hank raised his head and said, "He's down in Nashville, tryin' some big murder case and ain't expected back for several weeks."

Even though Loralie was crushed by the news, she patted Hank on the arm and said, "You tried and I thank ya kindly.

"What are you gonna do now? You can't go back up there by yourself and the only other lawyer here in town is the jasper that filed the papers for the Mullins, so he won't be no help."

Loralie looked out the window at the passing traffic and said, "I don't know, but I can't jest sit back and watch'm take my land and cut down my trees."

"They's at least nine or ten of them Mullins and they's tough, mean tempered men," Hank said, shaking his head.

The waitress brought their breakfast and they ate in silence. Outside, before they parted big Hank said, "You remember what I said, Missy, don't go off halfcocked. You get yerself some help if you plan on goin' back up there afore Henry gets back."

Loralie watched Hank lumber down the street in the direction of the blacksmith shop as an idea came into her head and she turned and headed for the telegraph office.

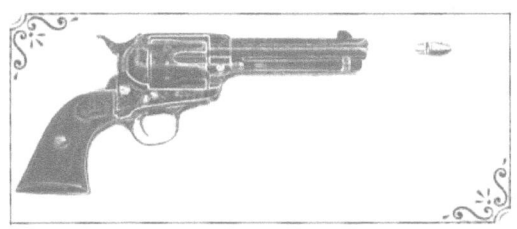

CHAPTER FIFTEEN

Clay thought he remembered seeing a small hospital close to the edge of town and rode in that direction.

At the hospital, Clay eased Lottie off the saddle and into his arms, marveling at how tiny she actually was.

A nurse saw a man coming through the doors with a woman in his arms, blood dripping from her back and leaving a trail on the floor.

The next thing Clay knew, Lottie was being taken out of his arms by two women who disappeared into a room, one of them yelling, "Serious gunshot wound, get the doctor!"

Clay was ushered to a small waiting room and given a cup of coffee. Shortly, another woman came in and began asking questions. Clay identified himself and told her what little he knew about Lottie and when he finished, the woman said she also knew of Lottie and wrote something on her papers, then left.

Clay was on his third cup of coffee when a short, rotund man of about fifty came in and introduced himself as Doctor

Thaddeus R. Michaels and told Clay that Lottie had died on the operating table. "The bullet glanced off her spine and did considerable damage to her insides. There was nothing I could do."

Clay thanked him and told the doctor he would pass the information on to the sheriff.

Clay didn't know what time it had been when he and Lottie escaped from the ranch, but it had been late. The moon was up and the sky filled with stars. It had taken him several hours to get back to town because of Lottie's condition, although he had pushed as hard as he dared. He figured it must have been somewhere around four when he got here. Add the time Lottie was in the operating room, it should now be somewhere close to five o'clock in the morning.

The restaurant had just opened when Clay walked in. The waitress took one look at him and brought him a cup of fresh, hot, black coffee. "You look like you've had a tough night. Did you win?"

Clay looked at her and asked, "Win? Win what?"

"You look like you've been up all night playing poker. It's either that or you've been riding all night. Which is it?"

Clay chuckled for the first time in quite a while. "You're right, I've been riding all night. I wanted to get here in time for the first cup of coffee."

"Sure you did. You want the special, steak, eggs, taters, fresh bread and coffee, fifty cents?"

"Are you a mind reader?" Clay said with a grin.

The waitress grinned at Clay. "Comin' right up, honey."

Clay sipped on the coffee and contemplated on what to do next. The bank money had been returned. Lottie was dead. The case was all but closed. Except for sending a few telegrams, his job was done and he could at last go home.

Clay was half finished with his breakfast when the sheriff came in and sat down at his table. "You've been busy."

When the waitress left with the sheriff's order, Clay filled him in with all that had happened, and when he finished, the sheriff shook his head.

"Don't worry about Lottie, I'll see to her. And, I'll see the judge and get a warrant for Grant Mouiser for murder. Course, you'll have to sign an affidavit saying Mouiser did it.

After Clay agreed to do that, the sheriff asked, "So what will you do now, wire for your next assignment?"

"Nope," Clay said with a wide grin. "After I send off ah couple of telegrams, I'm gonna get myself cleaned up, get some rest, then head for home. I got me a ranch I've been away from, far, far, too long."

The sheriff wished him luck, and left. Clay finished his coffee, then headed for the telegraph office.

After sending telegrams to his boss in Austin and the sheriff in Fort Smith, bringing them up to date, Clay boarded his horse at the livery stable, then headed for the hotel.

While his clothes were being laundered, he soaked in a tub of hot water to ease his aches and pains, then climbed into bed and was asleep as soon as his head hit the pillow.

Around four that afternoon, Clay was dreaming of riding the black stallion across a wide field of grass where close to a hundred horses were grazing and off in the distance was a large herd of cattle. The sun was shining; he was home, his place had been rebuilt and was up and running. Then, from somewhere off in the distance, he could hear a loud knocking noise and his name being called. He pulled the big stallion to a halt and listened.

"Clay! Clay - you in there? This is the sheriff. I've got a telegram for you from your boss down in Austin."

Clay pulled hisself awake, trying to figure out how he got in bed when he'd been out on the range? He stumbled to the door and opened it, glanced at the sheriff then staggered over to the washbasin, poured some water into the dish and splashed some on his face. He was wiping his face with the towel that hung on the peg next to the washbasin when it hit him. "Did you say you have a telegram for me from Austin?"

"I did," the sheriff said, handing him the yellow sheet of paper.

Clay sat down on the edge of the bed hoping this wasn't another assignment. He was tired and wanted to go home. He read the telegram, shook his head and read it again. "Good work: stop: You're a free man for now: stop: telegram from a woman – Clay, need your help, Cinch Mountain. Loralie Benson: stop."

"Sounds like this Benson gal got herself into some kind of trouble. You gonna go help her?" the sheriff asked.

"Do I have a choice?" Clay asked. "She saved my bacon once and I ain't one to forget. You happen ta know where this,

Cinch Mountain is?" Clay asked, standing up and grabbing his hat.

"I can show you on the map over to the office, but maybe you might think about getting dressed before you take off."

Clay looked down at himself and realized he was standing there in his underwear. He looked at the sheriff and shrugged his shoulders as he grabbed for his pants and began to put them on, both of them getting a good laugh.

Clay was lucky enough to make the train headed for Knoxville at six that same evening.

His horse was in a car all by hisself and Clay calculated with a short layover in Nashville he should be in Knoxville somewhere between eight and nine the next morning.

Clay sat at a table in the dining car, eating a light supper while going over things in his mind. Before leaving Memphis, he'd sent a lengthy telegram to his boss, Bill McDaniel, down in Austin, explaining as best he could about why he was going to Cinch Mountain, Tennessee. He ended the telegram by saying he would contact him as soon as he knew what the situation was.

Over coffee, Clay wondered what Loralie had gotten herself into that she would need his help; and could he get there in time? The telegram from McDaniel hadn't said when he got it, so he had no idea when she sent it.

Sipping on his coffee he told himself not to worry about something he had no control over, but that didn't help much. She was in over her head or she wouldn't have sent that telegram. He remembered her telling him about the Mullins.

Suddenly, Clay sat straight up. The doctor had said Lottie was dead, but he hadn't actually seen the body. Well, too late now to worry about it. It was the sheriff's problem now.

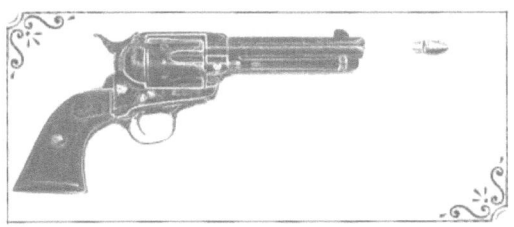

CHAPTER SIXTEEN

-

Loralie Benson left her horses in the cave, figuring they would make too much noise for the work she had to do.

With a pack on her back, she left the cave and headed for her old home site, the same place where the Mullins were camped. The moon was out and the sky was full of stars, which should give her enough light to work by. She giggled at the idea she'd come up with.

It took her over an hour, making her way through the forest to reach the spot she was looking for. She had been quiet and was sure no one had heard her, and she'd seen no one. Wearing moccasins she'd purchased just for this kind of work, she edged up behind a large tree where she could see their camp. The moon shone down on the camp and the only thing to be seen was the glow of the dying campfire. Loud snoring could be heard coming from the tents.

An hour later, Loralie moved back into the forest, and headed for the safety of her cave, satisfied with what she had accomplished. A dozen bear traps were hidden under leaves near their camp. They were all cocked and waiting for a victim. She knew the traps wouldn't stop them from cutting down the trees, but she hoped to slow them up some; at least until they could find all the traps. Knowing if there was one, there would be others.

Loralie was just edging up next to the boulder that hid the entrance to her cave when a loud scream echoed through the forest. It was a blood-curdling scream that caused her to stop and look back. "That's one," she said skirting around the boulder and into the cave.

After tending to her horses and eating a breakfast of pan fried bread, bacon and black coffee, Loralie checked her thirty-caliber, lever action rifle to make sure it was fully loaded, then put some shells in her coat pocket and headed back down the mountain.

She was sure they wouldn't do anything until it was light enough ta see. And even then they would go slow, poking a long stick out in front of them. Right now they would be seeing to whoever's foot had been caught in the trap. She hoped it had been ole man Mullin hisself.

Approximately a hundred feet from the clearing, Loralie stopped and looked up at the sky. Faint light was filtering its way through the tops of the trees. Daylight would be coming soon. She went down to one knee, keeping a low profile, then took a piece of jerky from her pocket and bit off a good-sized piece and began to chew.

Through the trees, she could see them moving around. The fire pit was ablaze and they were heating water for coffee. She would like to have a cup, but settled for water from the water skin hanging from her shoulder by a piece of rawhide.

Wilbur Mullin, one of the sons, came out of the center tent with ah bowl, not getting too close to the trees, afraid he might step on a bear trap, tossed out what looked like bloody water.

Wilbur was the youngest of the Mullin boys. He was probably around nine, she figured. He was no bigger than ah newborn colt and his eyes looked all around as he edged toward the fire and the pot of boiling water. It was easy to see he was scared.

Loralie stood up real slow like and with only part of her showing; she put the rifle to her shoulder and waited. Just as Wilbur reached for the ladle to dip some hot water into the bowl, Loralie squeezed the trigger, then disappeared back into the forest.

The bullet struck the pot with a thud, then hot water began to stream out into the fire, causing sparks to fly in all directions.

Wilbur jumped back like it was him that got shot. The empty bowl went one direction and he went in the other.

Immediately, six Mullin boys came charging out into the clearing, rifles in hand, looking for someone to shoot at, but there was no one to see.

When they realized what had happened, it was too late. The water from the boiling pot had put out the fire and most of the water had emptied out of the pot.

Ezra, one of the older boys, dressed in only his long johns and his hat, looked at the forest and yelled, "Who are you, and why are ya shootin' at us? Show yerself sos we can palver."

A bullet put a hole in his hat and he scrambled for cover. The others turned and shot in the general direction of where the shot came from, but all they hit were trees. Loralie had already headed for a different location.

She figured she was free to move around and take pot shots at her leisure, at least until they had cleared out the bear traps. None of them wanted to chase around in the woods with hidden bear traps waiting to be stepped on.

By nine that same morning, Clay had directions and was riding north toward the small community of S Mountain. He marveled at the difference of the land. Back on his ranch there were some hills, but nothing like where he was riding. The mountain rose up to a staggering height. The fact was, he couldn't see the top for the clouds that covered it up. He'd seen mountains in New Mexico and had seen the Rockies from afar, but this was his first time to venture onto an actual mountain. He and his wife, before she was killed, talked about going up into the Rockies of Colorado for a visit, but that seemed so long ago, now.

He knew from books the Rockies were taller than this mountain range, which made him shiver. Cinch Mountain had to cover more land than his ranch, his neighbors ranch and probably several others. If he remembered his history, Cinch Mountain was part of the Cumberland Mountain range where a lot of history had been made. A lot of the folks from Ireland had settled here and brought their music with them. And a lot of families had split because of the war between the North and the South. There had been brother against brother and even father against son. He was glad he never had to go. He didn't know which side he would have chosen; both had their points of view.

When Clay started up the road that led to the town of Cinch Mountain, he immediately felt closed in. One minute he was in the open and the next the sky was mostly blocked out by pine trees. The smell was enticing. It was a smell that made you feel good and he gave the big stallion his head and allowed him to set his own pace, which most of the time was a strong lope that ate up the miles, but this time it was slower. Going uphill was different than traveling across flat land.

As he rode, he wondered about a woman who would stand up all alone against a gang of cutthroats like she proposed the Mullins to be. Or was she alone? Did she just send for him so she would have another gun against them?

Riding through the forest gave him time to think about his life and life in general. Man had always been a predator as far back as the cave man. Even back then they were territorial and ready to kill one another at the drop of a hat. Why, he wondered, did man always seem to want what another man had? And what made a man a killer?

In his own case, it was first and foremost, anger; anger at Curly Beeler and his gang for raping and killing his pregnant wife, and secondly for shooting him and burning down his home and barn, then stealing all his stock.

He had always believed himself to be a peaceful man. In fact, he'd never even shot a pistol until the incident with Curly and his gang. And he'd only shot a rifle to bring down game for food.

But now, here he was, living by the gun and not proud of himself for it. But there were certain men and women who were different than normal folks. They robbed and killed without compassion; without regard for how their actions might hurt or even destroy other people's lives. It was those people that men like himself, had to stand up against.

As he rode along, Clay wondered if there would ever come a time when there would be no more wars, no more thieves and murderers, and would man ever evolve to live in peace with one another? He hoped it would, but if that should ever happen it would be many years down the road - far longer than he would live to see. Wouldn't that be something, never having to bar a door, lock a safe, or worry about people shootin' at you just because you looked at them wrong, or said something they didn't like. While the thought was noble, he doubted that man being what he is, it would ever happen.

It was late afternoon when Clay rode into the small community of Cinch Mountain. It wasn't much in comparison to Knoxville. Cinch Mountain was a bunch of buildings and a few houses that had sprung up because a town was needed here. Trees had been cut down and used to build the town, such as it was. It was as simple as that.

As he rode down the center of the street, on his left he saw as sign that said, Sheriff's Office and across the street a sign that read, The Water'n Hole. And further down he saw a restaurant and what looked to be a general store. At the far end of town there was a blacksmith shop that doubled for a livery stable, but nowhere did he see a hotel.

Clay reined in at the saloon and ground hitched the big stallion who wandered over to a watering trough and began to drink. Clay chuckled to himself, "Why not?" he said. "I'm about ta do the same thing."

Inside was typical of many other saloons he'd seen; only this one wasn't as big as most. The bar sat on one side of the room and the rest of the room was filled with six tables set up for drinking and card playing, or just sitting around jabber jawin'.

Besides the bartender, there were only two other men in the place. One was standing at the bar, sipping on a beer and the other was sitting at a table playing solitaire with a worn-out deck of cards.

The bartender looked up when Clay came in and stared at him as he walked up and laid his elbows on the bar.

"What'll ya have, stranger?" he asked without moving in Clay's direction.

"Got any cold beer?" Clay asked.

"Jest so happens, we do," the bartender said, reaching for a mug. "Be ah nickel," he said as he poured the beer from a spout behind the bar.

When he sat it next to the nickel Clay had laid on the bar, Clay noticed the sweat on the outside of the glass mug.

"Don't find many places that sell cold beer," Clay said as he lifted it to his mouth and took a sip. It was indeed, cold and tasted good.

"Just ridin' through, mister?" the bartender asked.

Clay wiped the foam from his lips and said, "Maybe. Lookin' to see some folks by the name of Mullin about buyin' some timber from them. Saw their advertisement down in Knoxville. Thought I'd see what they had ta offer."

The bartender eyed him with a crucial eye and said, "You don't look much like ah business man, more like ah cowhand or maybe ah lawman. You ah lawman, mister?"

Ignoring the question, Clay said, "And you don't look much like ah bartender, more like ah barber or maybe a mortician."

The bartender was tall and skinny as a rail and his eyes got big. "Ah mortician? Hell man I can't stand the sight of blood; makes me pass out sometimes."

The man just down the bar moved closer, but not too close and Clay noticed he had his holster tied down for fast drawing. The man was neither big nor small, medium height, maybe five foot nine or ten, slender build and wearing a suit that had seen better days. It was his eyes that Clay took notice of. They were mean, calculating eyes that bore through a man.

"You from Knoxville?" the man in the suit asked.

"No," Clay said as he took a longer pull of his beer.

"Where are you from, if not Knoxville?" the man pursued.

Clay turned and gave him a hard stare. "And what business of yours would that be?" Clay returned, staring hard right back at the man.

The man reached up and pulled the lapel of his coat back, revealing a star pinned to his chest. "I'm the law in this town and I make it my business to know about strangers."

"Well, then," Clay said with a grin. "If you would have said that in the beginning I would have been happy to provide you with the information you're looking for. My name is Fred Blackstone," Clay said, thinking on his feet, not wanting to reveal his real reason for being here, at least, not yet. Loralie had mentioned the sheriff, but something in his gut said to be wary. "I'm an attorney out of Wichita, Kansas and I'm thinking about opening a lumberyard. Wichita is growing and in need of good lumber, if I can buy it and ship it cheap enough…"

Clay knew if the sheriff wired anyone in Wichita about a Fred Blackstone, attorney at law, he would get a confirmation.

"What happened to the cowboy talk? All of ah sudden you… Oh, I get it, you come here lookin' and soundin' like some saddle tramp, thinkin' to bamboozle the Major, with some sob story about bein' down on yer luck and have very little cash."

"The Major?" Clay asked.

"Yeah, major. Silas Mullin was ah major for the confederacy back durin' the war. He's ah smart man and you've got yer hands full if'n you think ta slick talk'm."

Clay raised his mug for another beer, then motioned for the bartender to bring the sheriff another beer as well.

"Heard this Mullin fella took over some abandoned timberland."

The sheriff's eyes suddenly went cold. "What's that got ta do with anything?"

"Nothing, really," Clay said. "I just find it odd that someone with good timber like I'm told is there, would sell out instead of starting their own mill."

Their drinks came and the sheriff took a sip, then turned to Clay with a smile on his face. "Oh, that's easy ta explain. Ya see, ole man Benson and his wife was attacked by Indians and both of'm was killed. Their sons are out west somewhere, doin' god only knows what and the daughter, Loralie, she just up and abandoned the place some months back. Bein' ah woman she ain't got no head fer business, and well, the major, he laid claim and filed on the place and the judge deeded it over to him, all nice and legal like. Like I said, the major, he's smart and don't miss ah trick."

"I'll be sure to watch myself when I get down to dickering with him, then. Like you say, he's a smart man," Clay said, finishing off his beer and paying for the extra drinks.

At the door, Clay turned back. "How do I find this Major Mullin?"

The sheriff grinned and said, "Just head on up the mountain and he'll find you."

Clay took his horse down to the livery and saw to it that the black stallion got a good rub down and a full bate of grain and hay, then while making arrangements to sleep in the barn, he casually made mention of going up to see the major about purchasing some lumber.

"Take yer horse and get out," the holster said, picking up a hammer.

The man might be near sixty, but he was hard muscled, stood close to six feet tall and weighed close to two hundred pounds, but most disturbing was the look in his eyes that told Clay to back off.

"Whoa there, old timer. What did I do to set you off?"

"If'n you got anything ta do with them Mullins, then I don't want nuthin' ta do with you," he said, raising the hammer.

Clay and the holster stared at each other for a minute while Clay came to a decision that would either put him and the man on the same ground, or send him packing.

"What would you say if I said I was lookin' for Loralie Benson? I got a telegram from her sayin' she needed help, but I don't want anybody ta know why I'm here, yet," he said, taking the telegram from his shirt pocket and handing it to the holster.

The holster stepped over to the small room he used as a place to sleep as well as an office. A lamp set on the boards he called a desk. He turned the wick up until he was able to read the telegram.

He walked over and handed the telegram back to Clay and said, "I'm in. What can I do ta help?"

"Fill me in on what's goin' on. I need ta know everthing."

"First off, don't believe nuthin' that no good skunk of ah sheriff tells ya. He's on the Mullin's payroll."

They set in the holster's office, sipping on moonshine while he told Clay all he knew about the Bensons and the Mullins. "Ain't no doubt in my mind that it weren't injuns thet killed her folks. It was them Mullins thet tried ta make it look like injuns. I jest found out today thet she is back and tak'in it to'm all by herself."

He looked at Clay and said, "She might be only ah spit of ah girl, but them Mullins are gonna regret they got on her bad side, believe you me."

Before the sun came up the next morning, using directions the old holster gave him, Clay headed up the mountainside toward where the Mullins had staked a claim, while the old man rode off up the mountain to see if there were any Hackers about.

"If'n there's ta be any fightin', I know they'd want ta be in on it. Like most everbody else around here, they liked the Bensons. And they'd be plumb put out if'n they missed ah hoorah with them Mullins."

The trail was easy to follow as it wound up the mountain and Clay took note of the trees on both sides of the trail. "If this is any example of what Loralie's land is like, it's no wonder somebody would want to get their hands on it," he said to the black stallion.

There was a vast difference between the prairie land where he had his ranch and where he now rode. On his ranch, you could see miles of grassland where herds of buffalo used to roam, now dotted with herds of cattle and horses. The grass was tall and looked like ocean waves, swaying in the wind.

But here, thousands of trees stood like huge sentinels, guarding the land where their roots grew deep. Unlike the prairie, you could see only short distances. There were no buffalo here, but from time to time he saw deer standing still, looking at him. And once in a place where the mountain swelled out of the ground with giant boulders, he saw a mountain lion loping from rock to rock. The lion must have somehow sensed him for it stopped and looked down at him. He pulled the black stallion to a halt and they sat looking at each other until the lion decided Clay was too far away to be any danger, but hissed at him before disappearing into the upper reaches of the mountain.

Although he could only see the sky part of the time, he guessed it was close to noon when he heard the sound of horses coming behind him. He stopped the black stallion and glanced over his shoulder. Three men were riding hard in his direction and they had seen him, so there was no use in riding into the shelter of the trees.

Clay watched as the sheriff and two men rode up next to him and stopped. The two men looked rough and uncared for; both wearing tied down holsters and carried Winchester rifles across their knees. Neither one said anything, just sort of hung back, ready in case any trouble started.

"Mister Blackstone," the sheriff said. "I wired Wichita about you and I reckon you check out."

"Did you come riding all the way up here just to tell me that?" Clay asked, knowing the sheriff was up to something.

"Nope, not at all. We wanted ta catch up with you so we could make sure you didn't get shot. The major, he ain't too keen on strangers right now. But if he sees you ridin' with us, then he'll know it's alright."

"I see," Clay said as he turned the black stallion and headed up the trail.

"Right nice horse you got there, Mister Blackstone," the sheriff said, his eyes roaming over the black stallion like he was a young man looking at a pretty girl.

"You've a keen eye for horseflesh," Clay said, his eyes watching the trail ahead. He had an idea there was more to this than trying to make sure he didn't get shot.

An hour later they heard shots and the sheriff rode up next to Clay and grabbed the reins and then layed spurs to his own horse.

Clay glanced over his shoulder and saw that the two men with the sheriff were now riding with their rifles in their right hands, ready for use.

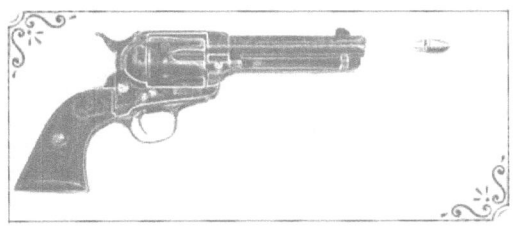

CHAPTER SEVENTEEN

-

Loralie sighted down the barrel of her rifle, held her breath and then squeezed the trigger with a smooth motion and watched as the heel of Brady Mullin's boot was ripped loose and went scooting across the ground.

Brady jumped like he'd been shot and lunged into one of the tents. Three rifle barrels came out through the flap firing blindly in all directions, while Loralie standing behind a large pine tree, fed a shell into her rifle and when the firing stopped, she lifted the rifle to her shoulder, again.

Her father and brothers had taught her well and she seemed to have a natural talent for shooting.

She sighted down the barrel, took a deep breath and squeezed the trigger. This time she watched as the rope holding the tent upright was torn in two and the tent collapsed on everyone inside, causing a lot of bellowing from ole man Mullin.

How long she could keep them at bay, she didn't know, but every hour was one hour more they wouldn't be cutting down her precious forest. She had plenty of shells and plenty of grub back up in the cave.

Loralie also knew ole man Mullin wouldn't stay hunkered down for long. He was a man who didn't like being opposed.

She watched from the shelter of the trees as they fought their way out from under the fallen tent. Silas Mullin stood up and looked around at the forest, his sons all holding rifles at the ready. Silas was a long drink of water, standing well over six feet. His slender build, had fooled many a man, thinking him to be weak. But that was just the opposite. He was tough and had a commanding way about him.

No one knew exactly where he'd come from, but like most folks people didn't know for sure about, there were rumors. One rumor was that he'd been a plantation owner who was burned out by the Yankees and joined the army for revenge, while another said he had been nothing more than a foreman on the Mullin plantation, who assumed the owner's name and title when the man was killed during the raid. Wherever the truth was, the man who called himself Silas Mullin had done a lot of physical labor that made him not only strong, but also tough as nails. Somewhere along the way he must have had some education too, for he had a reputation for shrewdness and had won several major battles against the north. It was said he was a friend of General Lee, himself, which may have had something to do with him being a major. But since no one knew for sure what the man's past was, it had all been purely conjecture. When Silas arrived on Cinch Mountain, he came with only his boys and, except for one, they were nearly grown. What had become of the wife, no one knew and he'd never spoken of it, and none of the boys had married, yet.

After a moment, Silas called out, "Who are you and what do you want?

Loralie stood in silence, not yet wanting to expose herself, even though the very core of her being wanted to yell at him to get off her property.

After a long silence, Silas called out, "What's the matter, you too scared to meet me face to face? You want something, come down here where I can see you, and we can talk. Hidin' up there like a coward is only gonna get you killed cause sooner or later one of us is gonna get you in our sights, then it's gonna be too late."

Loralie guessed he might be right, but still she remained silent. For the moment she had the upper hand and unless things changed, she could continue to harass him until she could figure out how to make them leave, if that was possible.

She put three rapid shots into the fire, throwing sparks in all directions and before they could recover, she'd moved back up the hill and off to her left to another sheltered spot where she could see them but they couldn't see her. They were out in the open, while she was hidden by the darkness of the forest and foliage.

They all had their rifles against their shoulders while their eyes searched the forest for someone to shoot at, but saw nothing but trees.

One of the boys ventured toward the edge of the clearing where he picked up a long stick and poked in front of him as he tried to enter the forest.

Loralie used the large rock she was hiding behind for a place to rest her rifle, and when he got close to one of the bear traps, she sent a slug down his way that embedded itself in the tree next to the man's head, causing him to back off. She wasn't ready for them to know where the bear traps were, yet, unless they happened to step on one.

He jumped back and fired his rifle into the forest, missing her by twenty feet.

"Stop that!" Silas yelled. "That's just what whoever it is wants you to do sos we use up all our ammunition."

"So you think it's a man up here, do you?" Loralie said to herself. "Don't reckon you can see ah woman with enough gumption to oppose ya. Well, afore long you're gonna be in a fit when you find out who has you treed down there."

Loralie was getting hungry and moved back silently and made her way back to the cave where her horses looked up when she entered. All was as she'd left it.

While Loralie was tending her stock and eating her lunch, unbeknownst to her, Clay, the sheriff and the other two men rode into Silas Mullin's campsite and hauled up. The place was in a mess. Two of them were in the process of putting a tent up and two others were cleaning up the fire pit area. Clay grinned. 'Loralie has been busy,' he thought to himself.

Silas walked over and looked up at the sheriff and asked, "What are you doing here and who is this stranger?"

"Mornin', Silas," the sheriff said as he stepped down and dropped the reins of his horse. Looking up, the sheriff nodded his head toward Clay and said, "He says his name is Fred Blackstone, from Wichita, Kansas, lookin' ta buy some lumber from you."

"That right?" Silas asked.

"That's what he says, only that ain't the truth. He ain't no more Fred Blackstone than I am General Lee."

"Then who is he?" Silas asked, drawing his pistol.

Clay looked over his shoulder and saw the two men behind him, pointing their rifles at him.

"Don't know," the sheriff said, "but we're gonna find out."

Clay was hauled off his horse and his pistol taken away by two of the Mullin boys.

"Who are you mister, and what are you doin' here?" Silas asked after slapping Clay across the face with the back of his hand.

Clay said nothing, but the look he gave Silas made Silas back up a step. Hastily, he turned to the sheriff and said, "Search him and see if he's carrying any papers."

Two of the Mullins grabbed Clay's arms and held him while the sheriff rifled through his pockets.

The first thing the sheriff came up with was Clay's Texas Ranger badge.

"Well, what have we here?" he asked holding the badge up for all to see.

"You're a bit out of your territory ain't you, Mister Texas Ranger?" the sheriff asked.

Clay stood absolutely still and said nothing.

The sheriff continued to go through Clay's pockets and found a telegram with Clay's name on it.

"Says here, his name is Clay Brentwood," the sheriff said holding the telegram toward Silas.

Silas slapped Clay's face again and asked, "Talk, damn you. What are you doing here?"

When Clay still didn't answer, the sheriff held up the telegram and said, "Says here that Loralie is back and askin' for his help."

"Loralie, here?" Silas said with a look of surprise on his face. "Yes. Now it makes sense. She's here alright, and making a bit of trouble for us."

"How so?" the sheriff asked.

"Well for one thing, she set bear traps out there in the forest. That's how I got this," he said, indicating his foot.

"How many did she set?" the sheriff asked.

"How the hell do I know? Ever time we try to venture out into the woods she takes pot shots at us!" Silas yelled.

Clay couldn't help himself and chuckled out loud.

Silas turned toward him and yelled, "You think that's funny, do you? Well we'll see how much you like it when we send you out there ahead of us to hunt the bear traps."

Everyone was shaking their heads in agreement and grinning at the thought of Clay stepping on a trap.

"And if I refuse?" Clay asked.

"Well then maybe I can help you make a decision," Silas said as he turned to one of his sons and said, "Get a rope and throw it over that limb yonder, then get a stump of wood for him to stand on."

Silas turned to Wilbur, his youngest. "Son, you go in the tent and look in the chest and bring papa's bull whip out here to me and I'll show you how we make our enemies talk."

They stripped off his shirt, and then tied his hands behind his back with a piece of wet rawhide, knowing it would shrink when it dried, thus, cutting off the circulation to his hands and making it very painful.

One of them threw a rope over a limb of a tree at the edge of the camp, and tied a hangman's noose in it, while another of them rolled a large piece of wood over and placed it under the rope.

Clay was shoved over next to the piece of wood, where the hangman's noose was slipped over his head and pulled taut. Next, he was lifted into a standing position on the piece of wood and the rope drawn tight, causing Clay to stand on the balls of his feet. The other end of the rope was tied to the trunk of the tree.

Clay knew full well if he fell off the piece of wood, the rope would either strangle him or break his neck. Either way, he would be dead.

Without warning, Clay felt the sting of the whip against his back, then heard the snap. Pain rushed through his brain like a tidal wave and it was all he could do not to scream. He didn't know about these hill people, but among the Indians, bravery brought a man high praise. And while he wasn't seeking praise, he wasn't about to let Silas Mullin hear him yell out.

When the second lash came, Clay bit down on his lower lip until it began to bleed, but still, he did not cry out.

"Tell me when you're ready to call it quits and go on back where you come from and I'll see you're cut free and given ah thirty-minute head start before I send the boys after you."

Would they give him a gun, a horse, Clay wondered, trying to decide what to do? The cuts were throbbing and he could feel blood running down his back. He had no reason to trust this man, but if he told him what he wanted to hear, at least maybe his back wouldn't be torn to shreds. It was apparent the man knew how to use a bullwhip.

How would he fare against men who had lived in these mountains their whole lives? He could see the lust in their eyes. He knew he must make a decision soon. He couldn't stand much more of this. The whip stung his back again and Clay's legs almost gave out on him. Not wanting to be hanged was the only thing that kept him upright. Where was Loralie? What was she doing? Did she even know he was here and what they were doing to him?

Loralie jumped as the first sound of the bullwhip being snapped reverberated through the trees. At first she wasn't sure what it was. It didn't sound the same as a gun being fired and when the second time she heard it, she jumped up, grabbed her rifle and ran down the mountainside. Somebody was being whipped, but who? Surely he wasn't whipping one of his own was he?

As the whip sounded for the third time, Loralie came up behind a boulder and could see Clay standing on a piece of wood with a noose around his neck.

"Oh, my God!" Loralie whispered to herself. Clay had come and this was the thanks he was getting. Silas was grinning, enjoying himself. "Well, what'll it be, boy? You gonna do as I say or do you want more of the whip?"

If you've never been stung by a bullwhip, it's like a thousand bees stinging you all at the same time. In the hands of an expert, the tip of the whip will cut long gashes in the skin, causing great pain, and Silas prided himself at being an expert with his whip. This wasn't the first man he'd brought around to his way of thinking and the few he hadn't, had died.

Without conscious thought, Loralie laid the rifle on top of the boulder and brought the butt against her shoulder. She could see the pain in Clay's face and her heart ached for him. This was not what she wanted when she had sent the telegram. How much more of this would he have to take? No more if she had any say so.

Clay was tempted to lie and tell Silas what he wanted to hear. He thought himself a tough man, but not sure how much more he could take without falling off the log. In the hands of an expert, and Silas considered hisself to be one, he could make a man's dying, long and painful. He saw the glint of metal in between two trees, just above a boulder. He let his eyes look around as far as he could, but no one else had seen it. He wondered if that might be Loralie up there? And if it was, what was she planning to do? He gritted his teeth and waited for the next sting of the whip.

She would need to make two fast shots and each had to hit a small target. She took a deep breath, sighted down the barrel and as Silas drew back his arm to let fly more pain, she squeezed the trigger, then swung the barrel over to her left and fired again.

The first shot hit Silas in the shoulder just as he was about to swing his arm forward. He screamed and dropped the whip, grabbing his shoulder. The second shot severed the rope just above Clay's head and he fell to the ground.

"Nobody move or the next shot will see somebody dead!" Loralie yelled. "You, Wilbur," she said, figuring him being young, he would follow her instructions without trouble, "Cut his wrists free, now or I'll kill yer pa!"

At the thought of his pa dying, young Wilbur pulled a knife from his pocket and ran over and cut Clay free.

Clay stood up, paying careful attention to not get between Loralie and any of them; he walked up behind Silas, turned him around and punched him in the face. " A Brentwood ain't so easy ta break," he said, then limped over and mounted his horse. His pistol belt was hanging from the saddle horn. He turned the horse in Loralie's direction and wondered how he would get through the bear traps when she yelled, "Everbody, turn around and keep yer eyes looking away from me. First one who don't gets ah bullet."

When they all had their backs turned to her, she ran down and took the reins of the black stallion and led him back up to the boulder. Once Clay was safe, she turned and fired a shot over their heads. "Everbody, face down on the ground! First one that moves will feel the sting of my rifle."

As soon as they were all face down on the ground, she led the black stallion on up the mountain toward her hideout, stopping every once in awhile to brush away any tracks.

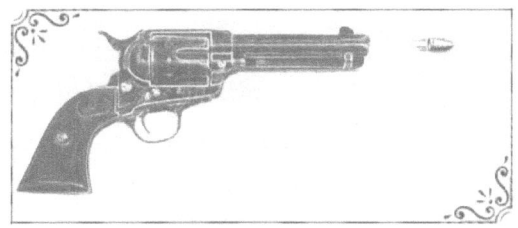

CHAPTER EIGHTEEN

Big Hank rode into the yard slowly, with his hands in the air. He hoped they would recognize him, but he wasn't going to take that chance. As he looked around, he almost chuckled to himself. Who was he raising his hands for; there was nobody in sight. Smoke rose from the cabin's fireplace but that was the only movement he could see.

"What you got yer hands up fer, Big Hank?" a familiar voice said behind him. Big Hank jumped like he'd been shot. He stopped his horse and looked over his shoulder.

Standing not fifteen feet behind him was John D. Hacker and within a blink of an eye, several more Hackers stepped out into the open, all cradling long guns in their arms.

"Climb of'n thet horse of your'n and come on in, coffee should be most ready by now. By the way, if'n you plan on sneakin' up on folks, you need ta quiet thet horse of your'n down ah mite, he clomps along like ah work horse. Heard ya comin' ah mile down the road."

Big Hank dismounted and one of the younger Hacker boys took his horse and led it to the barn where it would be cared for. Unlike a lot of city people, most mountain folk took care of what was important, and a horse was very important to them.

John D.'s wife Abigail looked up when they came in and immediately poured coffee in a mug and set a plate of sweetbread and a jar of sorghum on the table in front of where Big Hank was to sit.

"Land ah goshin'," Abigail said. "Ain't seen you in ah coons age. What brings you all the way up here?"

"I think he's bringin' news about that Benson gal," John D. said. Them Mullins stole her land from her and she went ta get it back, an I'm ah bettin' she's gone and got herself in trouble." He looked down at Big Hank and asked, "Am I right?"

Big Hank looked up, licking sorghum off his fingers. "Even more'n I expected, I reckon. Handlin' them Mullins all by herself was bad enough, but there was ah fella come ta town lookin' fer the Mullins. Tole the sheriff he was wantin' ta buy some lumber, but somethin' didn't set right with him and he sent off ah wire requestin' information."

Hank looked around the room and saw he had their attention. News of this magnitude was big and they didn't want ta miss ah thing.

"So, what did he find out?" John D. asked.

Big Hank took another bite of sweetbread covered with sorghum, chewed it slowly, took a sip of coffee then looked at them and said, "The feller he claimed ta be, weren't him a'tal.

The fella he claimed ta be was laid up with ah broke leg. Mister Timken, the telegraph operator tole me the man was really ah Texas Ranger by the name of Clay Brentwood."

John D. looked at his wife and said, "Remember me tellin' ya I run into that Benson gal jest the other day when I was off huntin'?"

"Yes. You said then you figured she was gonna get herself inta more trouble than she could handle and when you told her so, she said if'n she needed help, she'd holler."

"That's right. Thet's what she said." John D. turned back to Big Hank and asked, "So he showed up did he?"

Big Hank swallowed his third piece of sweetbread and washed it down with more coffee, then looked up and said, "Oh he showed up alright, but that ain't the half of it. Right after he headed out, the sheriff and two of his no-good friends lit out after 'em. You know thet the sheriff and them Mullins is in cahoots, don't ya?"

About then, Johnson Wallace Hacker came busting through the door, half outta breath. He sat down at the table and took the coffee offered to him, blew on it then took three sips before he was able to talk.

"Big trouble down at the Benson place.

"What kind of trouble?" John D. asked.

"Thet sweetbread sure smells good," Johnson said, looking kind of sad eyed at Abigail.

"Dammit man," John D. said, slamming his fist down on the table causing everyone to jump. "You can have all the sweetbread and coffee you want just as soon as you tell us about what's goin' on over ta the Benson place!"

JW, as he was mostly called, looked up and saw John D. staring at him intently. He cleared his throat and said, "I was needin' ah bit ah meat and I was followin' ah deer trail up above the Benson place and I heered some yellin' goin' on and well I reckon I got curious cause the next thing I knew, I was peekin' over this big rock and I could see Loralie leanin' against this here boulder with her rifle aimed down at some folks in the clearin'. It was the sheriff, two tough lookin' fellers and the Mullins. And there was this feller I didn't know, standin' on ah piece of log with ah noose around his neck."

JW took a swallow of coffee and continued. "Well sir, this here feller I didn't recognize was stripped to the waist and it looked like Silas had been layin' the whip to him. His back was all bloody and he looked about done in."

JW took another sip of coffee and before he could speak again, John D. asked. "What happened then?"

"Well now, if I hadn't ah seen it I might not have believed it, her not bein' ah Hacker. She whipped off two shots so fast it seemed almost like one. The first'n hit Silas in the shoulder and the second cut that hangin' rope plumb in two."

"Where are they now?" Big Hank asked, all wide eyed.

"She's got herself ah cave on up the mountain behind some boulders and brush. Best lil ole hideout you ever did see. I don't reckon I'd ah seed it if'n I hadn't follered her. She took that feller and his horse up to the cave. He was barely holdin' onta the saddle horn.

I reckon they's safe fer now, but sooner or later them Mullins are gonna find her. So I come over here. We gonna help her or are we gonna let her fight her own battles?"

John D. reached over and took his long rifle off the pegs where it rested on the wall, then grabbed up his bag of powder and shot. "She might not be kin, but them Bensons was always fair with us, and I don't like ah low down skunk that would treat ah woman like she's been treated by them Mullins. Besides, it's been too quiet around here lately."

CHAPTER NINETEEN

Clay nearly fell from the saddle when they reached the cave, but drawing strength from somewhere, maybe being just too stubborn to give up, he made it into the cave and sat down.

Loralie quickly made some tea from herbs she'd picked on the way back to the cave and while it was brewing, she cleaned the cuts on his back the best she could. She would need to cover them with something, but what? As a young girl, her mother had trained her in medicines. There were no doctors nearby so they had to rely on herbs, moss and other things that grew in the forest.

Suddenly she grinned for ear to ear. She wouldn't have to go lookin' for herbs, she had what was needed right here in the cave – honey. Earlier, on her way up the mountain, she had seen a hive and had harvested some. She liked a little in her coffee of a morning and on sweetbread when she had the time to make some.

The Cherokee woman that stayed with them from time ta time told her mama about honey. Not only did it cover the wound, but there was something in honey that killed all the germs and stuff. It was soothing and it left a much smaller scar from healing all moist like.

After covering Clay's wounds with honey, she made a cup of tea and handed it to him. He took a sip and coughed and gagged. "This is awful," he said in a weak voice.

She took a small sip and had to agree. After adding some honey and taking a sip, she handed it back to Clay and he drank it all down.

"I'm real sorry 'bout this," she said. "I never meant fer this ta happen."

"I know you didn't," Clay said weakly. The whip had cut him deep and he was in a lot of pain, but the poultice Loralie had put on his back was easing it quite a bit.

"You know it won't be long before they find a way through the traps and come huntin' for us. They can't let us live. You do know that, don't you?" Clay said matter of factly.

"This sure ain't the way I saw it in my head," Loralie said.

It was coming onto late afternoon. Black clouds were rolling in bringing with them heavy rain.

"Well, I doubt they'll be givin' us any trouble till this storm blows over," Loralie said with a spattering of relief in her voice. "How are you feelin'? Think you'll be up ta shootin' ah rifle when they come?" she asked.

Clay grinned and said, "Thanks to the honey on my cuts and that god-awful drink you concocted, I should be ready to take'm on all by myself, come mornin'."

"I really am sorry I…"

Clay held up his hand said, "No need ta feel sorry. I came of my own free will, knowin' there was gonna be trouble. My biggest mistake was not knowin' who the rotten apples in the barrel were. That sheriff is as crooked as the Arkansas river."

"I didn't suspect that, either. In fact, I trusted him, but I should'a know'd better."

Outside the rain was coming down so hard you couldn't see ten feet in front of you and anyone who tried to come up the mountain would have a rough time of it.

The Hackers and Big Hank hadn't gotten half a mile from their place when the storm hit and they were driven back.

"We'll hav'ta wait til mornin'," John D. said bending against the storm as they rode toward the shelter of the barn.

At the door of the barn Big Hank looked out, then turned and said. "Loralie and that Brentwood fella should be alright til tomorrow. Them Mullins ain't goin' nowhers, either."

Once the horses were wiped down and fed, they found pieces of canvas to use as a cover and ran for the cabin where they knew there would be food and hot coffee.

Abigail had heard them come into the yard and looked out the window, knowing they had to turn back due to the terrible storm outside. Earlier, she had seen the storm coming and prepared accordingly.

When they came in looking like drowned rats, she had pieces of cloth for them to dry off with and blankets to wrap up in while she dried their clothes in front of the fireplace. "Go in the other room and get out of them wet clothes so I can dry them by the fire, and after you're dried off you can wrap yerselves in the blankets on the bed. There will be ham hocks and beans, with fresh cornbread and plenty of coffee. You won't be goin' no place tonight."

John D. knew she was the right woman for him the day he met her six years ago come next Tuesday. He was down at the general store when she walked in. She'd given him no more than a slight smile and a nod, but that's all it had taken and six months later they had gone before the preacher, which he found out later was all her doin'. While she was ever much ah wife with all the cookin', cleanin', and what not, she was also a woman with a mind of her own and he liked that. Many a time she had seen the logic in somethin' he'd totally missed. And she liked him just the way he was and didn't try ta change him like some women he'd heard of did.

John D. knew Loralie was holed up in that cave of hers and she wouldn't have to worry about being attacked by the Mullins. Come first light, if the storm had passed, he and the others would ride down.

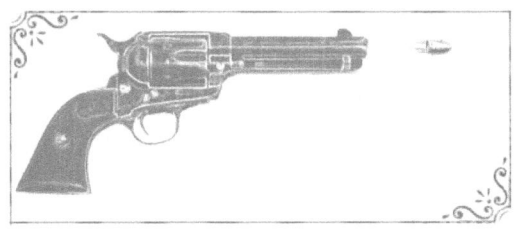

CHAPTER TWENTY

Loralie stood just inside the entry to the cave, near the side, where she would be in shadow and not an easy target, just in case someone was dumb enough to be out in this storm, but decided since she couldn't see morn' ten feet, neither could a shooter. She relaxed a bit knowing there wouldn't be trouble until morning.

Easing back inside, she saw Clay sitting upright drinking coffee. "We're safe for the time bein'. Even them Mullins ain't dumb enough ta try and find us in this weather. How you feelin'?"

Thanks to your fine doctorin', I reckon I'm gonna live. Only problem is, I'm indebted to you again. You saved my life down there."

"But you wouldn't ah even been there if'n I hadn't sent thet telegram," Loralie protested.

"Beautiful country," Clay said, changing the subject. "I can see why you'd not want ta give it up."

"Yes, I love the mountains," she said, looking toward the entrance of the cave. "And I suppose you love your wide open spaces," she said with a bit of apprehension in her voice.

Clay looked at her and realized how lovely she really was. Her red hair shone in the fire light and her smile was infectious. But he could also read in her eyes the anxiety she was dealing with. She was on the verge of losing everything she lived for, yet, she was ready to give her life to defend it.

Clay looked toward the entrance of the cave and wondered, was it all worth it? It was after all just a piece of land. Then he remembered his own land and knew he would go down fighting if someone tried to take it away from him. Clay looked up at Loralie who was standing with her hands on her hips, waiting for an answer to her question. Could he be happy here in her mountains, or could she be happy on his ranch, he wondered?

"Yes… yes, I do," Clay said, remembering riding over his own land. "A man can feel free out on the wide open spaces where you can see for miles out across your piece of the world, knowing it belongs to you."

Loralie sighed. "Up at the top of the mountain, I can look down and see the beauty of it; the trees, the animals who depend on it for their existence. There's wild berries and fish in the stream. It's my home. I guess I can't imagine livin' anyplace else."

Clay nodded his head. He had his answer. If they got through this, she would have her mountain and he would have his rangeland, and they would be friends, but the spread between them was too wide for anything else. They would both have to settle for that, which made him a little bit sad. He didn't like the thought of living alone.

By morning he would be strong enough to shoot and they would find out just how good he was with a rifle. It was no longer just her fight. After what they did to him, it was also his fight now.

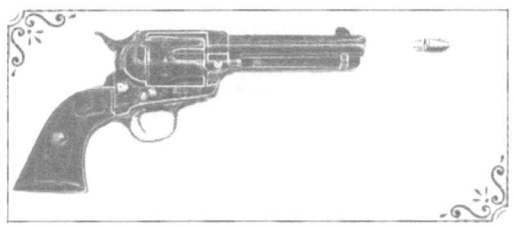

CHAPTER TWENTY-ONE

Silas Mullin paced back and forth in the tent, wondering if it was going to cave in due to the heavy rain and wind. It was leaking in several places and water was coming under the bottom, making the floor wet.

He was mad through and through. Why did she have to come back? She was spoiling all his plans. If she could have stayed away for a spell longer, he would have been ah rich man and wouldn't have cared if she wanted her land back. He would have taken what he wanted from the land and be living on easy street in some European city. Oh he would have given each of the boys a few dollars ta help them get ah new start somewhere, but the rest would be his and it would amount ta a small fortune. "Damn her hide!" he yelled.

Brady Mullin came ducking into the tent and hauled up, almost bumping into his father who was pacing back and forth. "What'cha thinkin' on, pa?"

Silas stopped his pacing and picked up a jug of moonshine and took a long pull, then handed the jug to Brady. "We'll be goin' after'm first thin' in the mornin'," Silas said, wiping his mouth with the back of his hand.

Brady set the jug down, wiped his own mouth, then asked, "How we gonna find'm pa? Thet storm out there has probably already washed away any tracks there might'a been."

Silas pulled a cigar out of the inside jacket pocket of his coat that was laying on the cot, and lit it with a stick from the small fire he had going close to the entrance to keep the chill off.

"She's got herself ah place up there somewheres," he said, waving his hand. "And she ain't goin' no place in this storm, either. She probably figures she's safe, but she ain't thinkin' straight. I know this mountain, too, and I have an idea where she's holed up."

The sheriff, who had been lying on one of the cots, set up and swung his feet down to the ground. "You plan on leavin' her and that other feller up there where you find'm?" he asked. "Knowin' Loralie, I suspect she'll have ah good place ta defend from and put up ah strong fight. How you gonna get around that?"

Silas walked over and opened a chest at the end of his cot, retrieved a stick of dynamite and held it up. "When I'm done with Loralie Benson and thet ranger friend of her'n, ain't nobody gonna be able ta find'm. And if'n she ain't around, there won't be nobody ta stop me from doin' what I set out ta do."

The sheriff eyed the dynamite and thought what a crafty old man Silas Mullin was. No wonder he was ah major in the war.

As he laid back down on the cot, he had a sudden thought. What did the old man intend to do about him? Would he shoot him in the back and claim Loralie done it? That way he wouldn't have ta pay him what he promised.

When the shootin' started tomorrow, he'd have ta make sure that the old man nor any of his sons got behind him. He pulled his hat down over his eyes, figuring he would be safe till then.

Snoring coming from under the sheriff's hat caused Silas to look in that direction and grin. "Come tomorrow, Mister Sheriff you won't be doin' no more snorin' cause you'll be dead, and that Benson gal will get the blame, either her or that ranger," Silas said to himself. "Won't make no difference which one gets blamed since you'll all be dead."

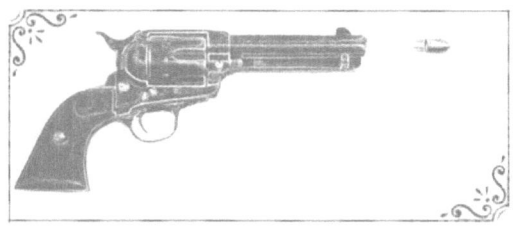

CHAPTER TWENTY-TWO

-

As the sun came up, Loralie was lying on her stomach, looking down the mountain for movement of any kind. She knew they would be coming just as soon as they found a way through the traps, which shouldn't take them long if no one was shooting at them. A slight breeze moved the tops of the trees, but all else seemed quiet. She was about to move back into the cave when a movement caught her eye. She froze, trying not to look directly at the spot where she'd seen movement. At first there was nothing. After nearly a minute, she saw it again and sighed. A doe moved into a small clearing, nipping the tops off a small bed of wildflowers.

She heard a sound behind her and looked over her shoulder. Clay was squatting next to the small, smokeless fire, pouring himself a cup of coffee.

"Feelin' better this mornin'?" she asked with a smile.

"Much better, thanks to your doctorin'," Clay said just before taking a sip of the fresh coffee. "And after a cup of this, I'll feel even better," he said raising the coffee cup.

"Think you'll be able ta handle ah rifle?" she asked, her eyes turning serious.

"Good enough," he said. "See anything?"

"Not yet, but they'll be comin' soon."

"My back is still ah mite tender, but hopefully I won't lyin' be on my back," he said, as he reached out an took his rifle from where it leaned against the wall of the cave. After checking to make sure it was loaded, he moved up to a spot close to the opening of the cave and laid the rifle next to where he would be shooting from. He, too, knew they would be coming and he wanted to be ready. He went to his saddlebags and retrieved a bag of shells and set them next to the rifle.

When he turned back, Loralie was next to the fire, fixing a breakfast of pan bread and bacon.

"I'll check the horses," Clay said, moving toward the rear area of the cave where the horses stood out of harm's way.

"Breakfast will be in about ten minutes," Loralie said as if fixing them breakfast was a normal thing to do.

Clay stroked the black stallion's neck and rubbed his back before giving each horse a bate of grain and some hay. A small basin in the rock held water for them to drink and Clay checked to see if it needed refilled, but decided there was enough for the day.

During breakfast, each was left to their own thoughts. Finally, over coffee, Loralie said, "I'm very sorry about what has happened. I reckon I shouldn't'a sent that telegram."

Clay looked over his raised coffee cup and said, "No one forced me to come. You knew you would be needin' help and I came because that's what friends do."

"But I should'a warned you about the sheriff."

"Did you know about him when you sent the telegram?" Clay asked.

"No… not really; not until I saw him with you and Silas."

"Then you couldn't have known, so stop worrin' about it and let's concentrate on what we're gonna do when they come after us. Can they come at us from up above?"

"I don't think so," Loralie said squinting her forehead. "It's at least ah hundred feet straight up the wall of mountain to the top and no way ta climb down. No. The only way they can come is straight up from the bottom and maybe off ta the sides, but between the boulders and the brush in front of the cave, there ain't no way fer them ta get ah clean shot until they get right up to us."

Clay moved over to the mouth of the cave and looked around, taking note of their position. It was good. They could shoot over the tops of the boulders and have a fair chance of hitting their targets, but shooting from the other way would not be so easy. Because of the boulders sticking up, they couldn't shoot into the cave and hope for a ricochet. But if they could get right up next to the boulders, they would have a chance.

"You know he can't afford ta let us live, not even the sheriff and the two men with him," Loralie said. He can't afford any witnesses."

Clay nodded his head as he looked for movement down below, but saw none.

Big Hank had the horses saddled and ready when the others came out of the log cabin. John D. came out carrying two sacks and handed one to Big Hank. "Vittles in case it takes us longer than I figure ta handle them Mullins."

Big Hank looked at the door of the cabin and saw Abigail standing there. He tipped his hat and said, "Thank you."

Abigail smiled and nodded her head as she watched them ride away, hoping to see them come riding back in soon. Them Mullins was grizzly bear mean and they had no love for the Hackers. But she also knew John D. was no greenhorn when it came to ah fight. All the Hackers she knew of were raised with ah rifle in their hands and when it came to a rough and tumble, they were as tough as there was in these here hills. She gave a sigh and headed for the yard, there were chores to be done.

Silas had been up several hours before the sun came up, thinking about where Loralie and her ranger friend might be. The girl was no stranger to this part of the country and would know ever place there was ta hide. It would be someplace where it would be hard for anyone ta get to, yet give her a clear field of fire.

He'd ridden this part of the woods hisself and thought he knew most of them, but she was raised here and would know all of them.

At the crack of dawn, he had them up and ready to go. No breakfast, just coffee and not too much of that. He wanted them in ah foul mood so's they would want to get this over with in ah hurry and get back.

"They'll be waiting for us," Silas said after seating himself on his saddle. "So, keep a look out for any movement. I suspect they'll be on a high up, hard ta reach position, with a better field of fire than we'll have, so stay ta cover as much as you can. And shoot ta kill! If either of 'em get out alive, we lose ever'thing."

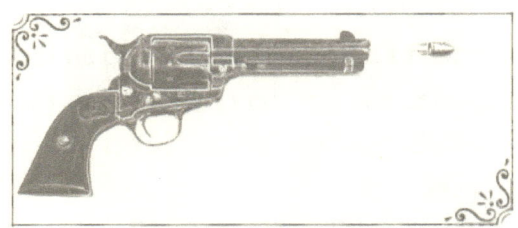

CHAPTER TWENTY-THREE

Henry Wadsworth Millstone rode his large, chestnut bay into town and went immediately to the livery stable to get an explanation about the telegram he'd received, only to find a young man he didn't know, tending the place. The young man said Big Hank told him he'd be gone a couple of days, but didn't say where.

After putting up his horse, Henry went to the restaurant. If anyone knew what was going on, Sonya would. She never said much but people talked and Sonya listened.

Sonya greeted Henry with a large smile, a cup of coffee and a large slice of Dutch Apple pie.

When he asked about Hank and this Loralie woman, Sonya nodded her head and since they were the only ones there, she pulled up a chair and sat down.

Ten minutes later, Sonya said, "And now you know as much as I do. But I've got a bad feeling deep down inside. Them Mullins are trying to steal her land."

Henry admitted he'd never met any of the Mullins, but he'd sure heard plenty of stories.

He patted the inside pocket of his coat and said, "I've got papers right here to prove Miss Benson owns the land. Her father had the good sense to record it."

"I suspect you'll need to get up there as soon as you can," Sonya said. "I'll fix sandwiches."

"Yes, I'll take the sheriff with me to make sure they understand," Henry said, standing up.

"Sheriff's already up there, 'cept he's on the Mullin's payroll, so he won't be doing you much good," Sonya said with a sigh.

Henry stood outside the restaurant and looked around, wondering what to do. He saw the saloon and headed that way. Inside, he saw at least a dozen men, some of them he knew. He walked up to the bar and told the bartender to set up drinks all around. The men hastily bellied up to the bar and when they had their drinks, he said, "I understand the Mullins have taken over the Benson place."

All the men nodded their heads and the bartender leaned on the bar and said, "It's a shame. They say Loralie can't prove the land belongs to her cause the papers were burned up in the fire, so I guess the Mullins will take possession whether she likes it or not."

"Not necessarily," Henry said.

"Whata'ya mean, not necessarily?" one of the men asked.

Henry pulled a piece of paper from his coat pocket and laid it on the bar. "As those of you who know me, know I'm an attorney and I just happened to be in the capital trying a case when I got a telegram from Big Hank."

The room was silent as the men stood waiting for further explanation.

"I went to the records department and got a copy of the title, showing it is still owned by the Bensons. And that's it right there," he said pointing at the piece of paper.

There were cheers all around until Henry raised his hand. "I understand she went up there to try and talk the Mullins into leaving, but you and I know that he won't give up without a fight, and as I understand it, there is only her, a Texas Ranger and Big Hank."

Adding his two cents worth to the conversation, the bartender said, "I wouldn't count on the ranger much. The sheriff and two of his men lit out after him shortly after he left town."

"Yes. That's what I understand," Henry said, setting his glass on the bar. "That is exactly why I'm here. I need men to ride with me when I go up there and serve Silas Mullin with eviction papers. I'll pay ten dollars a day."

The bartender pulled off his apron and was the first man to sign on.

Within thirty minutes Henry and thirteen men were riding toward the Benson property, all of them armed and ready for war.

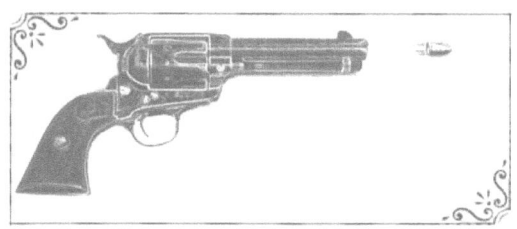

CHAPTER TWENTY-FOUR

John D. hauled up when he heard rifle fire coming from down below. He looked at Big Hank and said, "Sounds like they've started the dance without us."

Big Hank grinned and said, "Then I guess we'd better be makin' tracks!"

Being men who knew the mountain, they were able to ride at a good clip, zig-zagging in and out between the trees.

Clay saw Silas and his people coming and put a bullet into one of the men's leg. The man let out a scream as he left his horse and fell to the ground.

Suddenly the air was filled with gunfire, all of it coming from below. Lead was hitting the mountain all around the cave, but none had found its way inside.

Loralie said, "Save yer ammunition till you can get ah good shot."

Clay grinned and said, "Yes ma'am," then turned his attention back to the forest. This was serious business and those men down below had come with killin' on their minds.

Clay caught a glimpse of a reflection off the barrel of a rifle. It was laying in the vee of a small tree, and pointed up toward the cave. Clay took careful aim and put his bullet just above the barrel, the sound reverberating off through the trees.

The rifle barrel disappeared from sight, but there was no scream of pain.

Silas looked over and saw his son, Angus, lying on his back, a small red spot in the middle of his forehead. His eyes were cold and dead.

"Damn your eyes, Loralie Benson!" Silas yelled, his voice filling the mountain air.

John D. Hacker, Johnson Wallace Hacker, and Big Hank, heard Silas's yelling and realized they weren't more than a quarter of a mile from where the fight was taking place. They turned in that direction and headed off in a hurry as gunfire continued to fill the air.

Silas was wild with anger. One of his sons was wounded and another one dead. He wanted to kill Loralie Benson himself. He wanted to watch her suffer, as she died a slow miserable death. He was a man with no other thought than to kill his enemy, Loralie Benson. Climbing aboard his horse, he kicked the animal in the sides with his spurs and rode hell bent up the mountainside, firing his pistol.

Both, Loralie and Clay watched Silas emerge from the trees. The man was no longer in control. His eyes were wild with hate. Clay pulled his rifle to his shoulder.

"Don't kill him," Loralie said with a quietness that caused Clay to look in her direction. "He's already dead, inside."

Clay turned back and sighted down the barrel of his rifle. The bullet caught Silas in the right shoulder joint and knocked him from his horse. Silas dragged himself behind the nearest tree and safety, his pistol still out in the open, too far to reach.

The silence that followed was intense. Finally, the sheriff called out, "Surrender now and we'll let you live."

His answer was a bullet from Loralie's rifle that tore a piece of bark from the tree he was hiding behind. The man she thought her friend was now her enemy and she knew he was lying. He had to kill her and Clay, he had no other choice.

The piece of bark flew past the sheriff's head causing him to duck. Moving over behind another tree, he yelled, "Get the dynamite!"

Bullets were ripping the mountain all around them as the others laid down cover fire for the sheriff as he ran out of the trees and threw a stick of dynamite in their direction. It hit the top of one of the boulders and rolled off onto the backside.

The explosion disrupted the boulder and sent it hurdling down the mountain to where it slammed into the wall of trees, leaving a clear path to the cave with Clay and Loralie now exposed to their enemy.

Bullets began slamming into the walls of the cave, causing Loralie and Clay to hug the front side walls hoping to not get hit by a ricochet bullet.

Loralie looked over at Clay and said, "I'm sorry," then jerked as a bullet bounced off the wall of the cave and drove its way into her side. "I'm hit," she yelled and turned back toward the men shooting from below, trying to line up a shot, but a second bullet hit the edge of the opening and threw dirt and rocks into her face.

With the sheriff leading the way, they advanced from tree to tree until they were close enough to be sure of a victory. Loralie and the ranger were trapped in the cave and had no way out without making targets of themselves.

The sheriff eased up next to Silas, who had retrieved his pistol. "We don't need to waste any more bullets or chances of getting shot," the sheriff said. "From here, I can throw a stick of dynamite into the cave and get rid of them once and for all."

Silas looked at the sheriff and grinned. "You've got ah head on yer shoulders, son. Too bad you gotta die too."

The sheriff looked at Silas, then his eyes went wide as he felt the bullet slam into his stomach. For just a moment, he was stunned, then things went black as the second slug took him in the heart, knocking him backward. His cold dead eyes stared up at Silas without seeing him.

Silas's other son, Ezra, came running over, holding a stick of dynamite in his hand, the fuse burning.

"Aim true, boy, aim true," Silas said, motioning toward the cave.

"I will, pa. I surely will," he said as he raised his arm and threw the dynamite with all his strength.

The stick of dynamite landed on the floor of the cave in between Clay and Loralie.

Without thinking, Clay crouched and ran to Loralie, kicking at the stick of dynamite as he went. His foot hit the dynamite and sent it back toward the opening of the cave, but not far enough. Clay picked up Loralie and carried her back into the cave, hoping to escape the blast. They were deep into the cave when the dynamite exploded. In a loud roar and a cloud of dust, the entrance to the cave disappeared, sealing them inside.

About this same time, John D. Hacker and the others rode out of the trees. John D. saw Silas and yelled, "Hold it right there, Silas. We got you covered, you land grabbin'…"

Silas looked over and saw them, but he was still too far gone to think rationally. He was too close to succeeding with his plan to give up now. "Kill them," he yelled, lifting his pistol and pointing it at John D. Hacker.

John D. pulled iron and shot both, Silas and his son who was standing next to his father with his pistol pointed at them.

Big Hank and JW both had their pistols trained on the other two.

Young Wilbur and his older brother Samuel dropped their rifles and held up their hands, along with the sheriff's two men.

Before he died, Silas looked up at John D. and said, "You may ah killed me, but Loralie Benson and her ranger friend are goin' ta hell with me. They're buried in that cave up yonder an I hope they die ah slow, painful death."

Big Hank was the first one up there, tossing rocks out of his way, digging with his hands. How much rock and dirt he had to dig through he didn't know, nor did he know if he could find them alive, but he had to try.

Inside the cave, next to the dying embers of the small fire, Clay laid Loralie down and then pulled her shirt up enough to see the bullet wound on her left side. She had other scrapes and abrasions, but they were minor and could wait. The first thing he had to do was to get the bullet out of her. She was unconscious and her breathing was ragged and shallow.

In the semi-light from the coals Clay added sticks to the small fire and laid his knifepoint in the hot coals, then gently as he could, felt her side and found where he thought the bullet had lodged itself.

"Please understand, Loralie, I don't aim to hurt you, but a doctor in Knoxville is as close as there is, and if I don't get the bullet out now, you might not make it."

Somewhere in the recesses of her mind, Loralie must have heard him and she opened her eyes.

She reached up with her right hand and drew Clay down next to her face, then kissed him and said, "Just do what ya gotta do," then turned her head.

When the hot knifepoint dug into her flesh, she couldn't help herself and she screamed.

Henry and his men had just ridden up and were running toward where Big Hank was digging with his hands and Henry asked, "Is Miss Benson in there?"

Hank nodded and said, "Her and the ranger. They may still be alive! We gotta gett'm out!"

When they heard Loralie scream, Henry dropped to his knees and began to dig for all he was worth, trying to help Hank make the hole larger.

"You folks alive?" Big Hank yelled, as he made a small opening in the dirt.

"Barely," Clay's voice answered. "Loralie has been shot!"

They were careful to make the hole big enough to get Clay, Loralie, and the horses out safely, but not big enough to cause it to cave in.

With both, Hank and Henry digging, they had them out in less than thirty minutes. Big Hank was hovering over Loralie, checking her wounds, while John D. was checking Clay. When he saw the wounds on Clay's back, he whistled and asked, "Silas?"

Clay nodded, just before he passed out.

Two days later, they were all having dinner at the restaurant in Knoxville. The ownership papers had been filed giving Loralie possession of her property again. The doctor had bandaged her side and took care of her other wounds; including a large gash on her head from the cave in. He told them she would be as good as new in a week or so.

The doctor also said the honey had been the best thing for Clay's wounds as he put a new dressing and bandage on Clay's back, and dressed his other cuts and abrasions.

During this whole time, Henry had fussed over Loralie like she was royalty.

Liking his attention, Loralie smiled and laughed at almost everything Henry said.

Sitting across the table from them, Clay suddenly wondered what had happened to Wilbur and Samuel Mullin? The last he'd seen of them was up on the mountain. He turned to Hank and asked him about them. Hank smiled and said they had slipped off into the forest. He hadn't said anything because he figured they would never be seen or heard from again.

He heard Loralie's laughter and turned his head in her direction.

It didn't take Clay but seconds to see what was going on between her and Henry. Their eyes lit up whenever they looked at each other.

At one point, Loralie looked across at Clay with sorrow in her eyes, then back at Henry and her heart had mixed feelings. She was a mountain girl and Henry was Tennessee born and loved the mountains – he'd told her so. Loralie looked over at Clay and sighed. He was so strong and handsome, but he was a flatlander. She wanted to talk to him and explain, but Henry said something and she turned back. Henry was not only handsome, but he was book learned. He was an attorney.

On one hand, Clay was glad for Loralie. He figured Henry would make her a good husband, but on the other hand, he also wondered what it might have been like if the circumstances had been different.

Well, it was too late now. It was obvious what Loralie wanted and he knew what he needed to do - go home and rebuild his ranch.

Clay stood up and said his goodbyes all around, then headed for the door, a train headed west would be leaving in less than an hour and he needed to be on it.

Loralie felt a pain in her chest when Clay took her hand and said goodbye. His touch sent shivers up and down her spine, and when he turned to leave, she almost jumped up and asked him not to go.

Was she doing the right thing? Did he feel about her the way she felt about him? She thought he did by the way he looked at her and the way he always seemed to be there when she needed him, but mainly, the way she felt when he touched her. Why did things have to be so complicated?

A few minutes later, when Loralie heard the sound of the train whistle as it left the station, her breath caught in her throat and tears began to run down her cheeks.

To the surprise of everyone at the table, Loralie jumped up and limped out of the restaurant, as fast as she could.

THE END

Thank you to all my readers. Your reviews and requests for more Clay Brentwood books is an inspiration to me. I'll keep writing them as long as you keep requesting them...

MEET THE AUTHOR

JARED McVAY is a four-time award-winning author. He writes several genres, including - westerns, fantasy, action/adventure, and children's books. Before becoming an author, he was a professional actor on stage, in movies and on television. As a young man he was a cowboy, a rodeo clown, a lumberjack, a power lineman, a world-class sailor and spent his military time with the Navy Sea Bees where he learned his electrical trade. When not writing you can find him fishing somewhere or traveling around and just enjoying life with his girlfriend, Jerri.

THANK YOU FOR READING!

If you enjoyed this book, we would appreciate your customer review on your book seller's website or on Goodreads.

Also, we would like for you to know that you can find more great books like this one at

www.SixGunBooks.com

Stories so real you can smell the gunsmoke.™